Tequila & Lace

By Kimberly Knight

Tequila & Lace

Print Edition

Published by Knight Publishing & Design, LLC

Cover art © Okay Creations

Cover Photographer © by E. Marie Photography

Dedication

To the original Paul Jackson.

There is rarely a day that I don't think of you. I miss you too much.

May you rest in peace.

Chapter One

Joselyn

I stared out of the tiny, grungy, living room window of our two-bedroom mobile home. Today was my birthday and for the past seventeen years, I couldn't remember a birthday when I'd woken up to presents and cake, or even my mother wishing me a happy birthday.

Today was no different.

"When are we gonna have cake?" my brother, Bryce, asked, tugging on the hem of my purple tank top.

I turned and looked down at him. I didn't know if we were going to have cake at all, so I did my best not to give him false hope. "I'm not sure, buddy. Maybe when Mommy wakes up."

"But I want cake now!" he whined, crossing his arms over his chest and sticking his bottom lip out.

I wanted to tell my eight-year-old brother that I wanted cake now too, but we didn't have money to go to the store. There was also no way I was waking up Mother in hopes she'd remembered my birthday—even if it was close to two in the afternoon.

"How about you draw me a cake and by the time you're done Mommy might be awake? You haven't given me my present yet." I reached out and ran my hand over the top of his hair, messing up the shaggy light brown length that was opposite of my dark brown. I knew I was only biding time, but once Mother was up and in one of her moods, he'd forget about the cake and watch cartoons instead to avoid her antics.

"Fine," he huffed, then turned on his heels. I watched as he ran down the hall toward the room that we shared. I silently prayed he didn't wake Mother. If he did, she'd yell and make him cry, then leave me to get him to stop. She was still asleep because she worked nights. I'd thought she worked as a waitress at an all-night diner or something, but when I was thirteen, I learned the truth. I'd woken up as she was coming home at four in the morning dressed in a red tube top, a short black skirt that barely covered her panties (*if* she were even wearing any), black fishnet stockings, and black high heels that I was certain would cause me to break an ankle.

"What are you doing up?" she asked, narrowing her eyes and glaring at me as she closed and locked the small, metal trailer door behind her.

I swallowed. "I… Uh… I'm getting some water."

"Hurry up and get back in bed, Joss." She brushed past me as she made her way down the narrow hall toward her bedroom. She smelled of cigarettes and sweat. All traces of her perfume I'd seen her squirt on her wrists before leaving were gone.

"Why are you dressed like that?" I asked. She had been wearing jeans and a T-shirt when she'd left the house, so I was curious, but I quickly regretted the question as she spun on her heels, anger flashing in her eyes. She backtracked toward me, pointing her index finger.

"I'm the adult. You don't get to question me."

I huffed. She'd left me alone every night for as long as I could remember. Luckily, I had Mrs. McKenna next door if anything were to ever happen to my brother and me. "You're dressed like—"

"Like what, Joss?" She put her hand on her hip and cocked it when she was a few feet from me.

My eyes widened. I should have known not to question her. Whenever I did something she disapproved of, she'd whip me with a flyswatter, a wooden spoon, a belt, a shoe—whatever was on hand, and I didn't feel like crying myself to sleep if she decided to ever use the end of her spiked heel.

"Like what, Joss?" she asked again. I wasn't sure, but it didn't sound as if she were surprised by my question, or that she wanted to hide something.

I took a quick deep breath before I spoke. "A… Uh, a hooker."

I'd expected her to reach down, slip off her heel and throw it at my head. Instead, she'd laughed while her eyes closed briefly. She shook her head, not necessarily telling me I was wrong. "I really didn't want to have this conversation at four in the morning, but you're bound to find out at some time." She motioned for me to sit at the light blue card table we used as a kitchen table as she lit a cigarette. I watched the smoke float in the air before she spoke again. "Yes, I'm a hooker."

Have you ever had one of those moments where your world felt as if it were spinning on its axis? Or as if your head were spinning on your body? Even though she dressed as a hooker, and she worked crazy night hours, I hadn't suspected that my own mother was a prostitute.

"Are you going to say something?"

My eyes focused on her face as I realize I was staring at her, trying to wrap my head around what she'd professed. What were my friends at school going to think if they found out? "So you like… stand on the corner?"

She blew a poof of smoke into the air above our heads. "Gotta make money to feed us and put a roof over our heads somehow."

"Why a hooker? Why not a waitress or something?" During the summer, Mrs. McKenna's grandson, Seth, would visit. We'd play house with my friend Catherine (or Cat as we called her) and choose professions like a doctor, lawyer, teacher, bank teller, waitress, housewife, but never a hooker. Seth was always a cop. He was four years older than us and wanted to protect us from all the bad guys.

She chuckled. "If your father hadn't left us before you were born, we wouldn't be living in a dump, Joss. I got pregnant when I was your age and your grandparents kicked me out for getting knocked up. I thought your father would take care of me. Instead, he left me at a gas station in the middle of nowhere between here and Fort Lauderdale.

"I didn't know what to do or where to go. I thought your father loved me. I thought he wanted to be with me. I was young and stupid and so wrong. Luckily, I met Tony at a diner I'd walked to. After he'd bought me some food, he drove me here to Miami and gave me a room in his house. Long story short, after I had you and was able to have sex again, I started working for him."

I hadn't asked many questions after that. I didn't want to know what was going on when she left the house. I kept her *profession* a secret, even after Seth became a cop in D.C. Mother mentioned recently that her *duties* had changed a little—I still didn't ask questions. All I knew was she dressed more business-like now. Her skirts were a little longer and her shirts covered more of her torso. She seemed happier but continued to put Bryce and me on the back burner.

Every night was the same. She left around four in the afternoon, and I stayed home to feed Bryce, made sure his homework was finished and put him to bed at a decent hour. On school days, I took him next door to Mrs. McKenna's before I took the bus to school. *She* was the one who took him to school and picked him up when it was over because Mother was sleeping at those hours. I wasn't sure if Mrs. McKenna knew what Mother did for a living, but I wasn't going to tell her. I felt terrible that she cared for a child who wasn't her own, but I saw the love in her eyes when it came to him, and I was only a kid myself. I had no other choice.

Now I only had one more year until I was an adult. I wasn't sure what was after high school for me. I didn't want to stay home and take care of Bryce. I loved him, but I wanted to get a job, save up money, and move out on my own. I wanted to be roommates with Cat, go to parties and live wild and free. But I knew college wasn't in my future, not even community college. I wasn't sure if I'd be able to afford my share of the rent, pay bills and obtain a degree. Hell, I didn't even know what I wanted to be when I *grew up*.

As I stared out the window, thinking about my future and the year to come, there was a slight knock against the screen of the front door. "Mrs. McKenna," I greeted. I always used her formal name. It was how I was introduced to her and it had stuck.

"Happy birthday, dear. You have a phone call." She smiled and reached her hand out to pass me her cordless house phone. "I'll watch Brycie. Go ahead and use my phone inside." She motioned with her head toward her trailer.

I took the two steps down while holding the screen door so it didn't slam and wake Mother. "Thank you." I beamed and switched spots with her, then walked a few feet away before speaking into the phone. "For my eightieth birthday, please tell me you'll show up and not just call?" I chuckled as I stepped into the other trailer that was less than twenty feet away.

Seth's mature voice rang through as he spoke. Over the years, I'd heard it change into a deep *manly* voice and now it did things deep in the pit of my belly that made me grin like a complete fool whenever we spoke. "I'll show up as your knight in shining armor. Should it be on a white or black horse?"

I laughed again. "How about a white or black car?"

"I could do that if I picked you up at the airport here."

"Oh my God. I could just see the look on people's faces as I got in the back of a D.C. squad car."

"Want me to handcuff you too?"

"No way!" For a split second, images of being handcuff naked with Seth kissing his way down my body flashed in my head. Teen hormones were no joke, but I was waiting. I wasn't sure if I was waiting to be with Seth when I turned eighteen and legal—since he was a cop and twenty-one, or if I was waiting until I found someone *special.* All I knew was I didn't want to treat sex like my mother did.

"I'm only joking, Joss."

I smiled as I envisioned him smiling on the other end. I loved his smile. When he did, his mouth curved enough to cause his cheeks to meet his eyes, and when they squinted, you knew you had a genuine smile out of him. I knew at that moment—on the other end of the phone—he was giving me that smile. We were silent for a few beats as

I looked around at the pictures of Seth from his childhood that were scattered throughout the small living room.

"It's actually white."

"What?" I asked, my eyebrows scrunched in confusion.

"The squad car. It's white with red decals and blue writing."

"Oh. Well, I've never been on a plane before. Not sure if I'd even make it up to see you."

"You've never been on a plane?"

I frowned. "Nope." I'd actually never left the trailer park for more than one night.

"All right. For graduation, I'm taking you somewhere on a plane."

I sighed and fell back onto the cream colored velvet couch with burnt orange roses. "Aw, man. I gotta wait over a year?" I was teasing, but getting away sounded like heaven, especially with Seth.

"Not my fault you're a baby. We gotta wait to get you an I.D. so you can go places since Cruella won't let you get one."

"I have my school I.D."

"Tempting, but you're still a baby."

I rolled my eyes. "And you're still an ass."

"Not my fault you don't have an older brother. I have to step up." I cringed at the word brother. "Anyway, birthday girl, I gotta go. Duty calls and all that shit—"

"Yeah, yeah, go catch those bad guys."

He chuckled. "Have Grandma cook you something good for dinner. You know she will."

"I know," I sighed. "I just want cake." *And candles … And to make a wish as I blow out the candles.*

"She'll bake you one, Josie. She makes a mean 'better than sex' cake."

"Come again?" I covered my mouth with my hand as the words spilled from it. *Sex. Cum. Talking to Seth about sex and cum. Fuck my life.*

"It's a chocolate cake, Joss. And it's fucking awesome."

"All right. Go catch those bad guys and I'll just be over here having an orgasm while I eat cake." I hung up the phone before he could respond. I wanted the last word and I wanted him to think about me having an orgasm … even if I was a *baby* in his eyes.

Fucking teenage hormones.

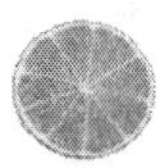

After placing the phone back on its cradle, I returned to my trailer. Mother was still asleep and Bryce was just coming out of our room, running with a sheet of binder paper in his hand.

"Shh, B, you're gonna wake Mom." I gave Mrs. McKenna a tight smile after I lifted my finger to my mouth.

"I drew you a birthday cake," he whisper-shouted.

"I love it," I whispered back and took the paper from the palm of the hand my mother had used as an ashtray.

I was thirteen and Bryce was only four. Mother had the night off from her job, which was rare, and we were watching 101 Dalmatians. We didn't have cable and the only VHS cassette we owned was the cartoon from 1961, so we knew this movie by heart. I hated when she was home because she was usually pissed off at us, and she'd end up passed out on the couch after drinking a bottle of gin. This night was no different. She was angry at Bryce for something that was "all his fault" and he was crying. Before I knew what was happening, she'd yanked his hand and used it as an ashtray. I rushed him over to Mrs. McKenna's trailer, telling her he'd burned it on the stove. She bandaged his hand, and when we returned home, Mother was passed out on the couch. The next few months, Mrs. McKenna made sure to check on us nightly.

"Want me to bake you a cake?" Mrs. McKenna asked.

"That won't be necessary. She won't be home."

My eyes darted toward the hall as my mother came around the corner, tightening her belt on her baby blue robe around her waist. "I won't?" This was the first I heard about it.

She shook her head. "You have plans."

We never had plans; especially plans for my birthday. "*We* do?"

"Yes." Her tone was short, so I wasn't going to question her again.

"Well, then I will let you get to your plans," Mrs. McKenna remarked, reaching for the front door.

"Thank you again." I gave her a quick hug. She nodded to my mother then left.

"What was that all about?" Mother asked, a cigarette between her lips as she flicked her lighter. I watched as the flame burned the tip.

"Seth called to wish me a happy birthday."

She blew a puff of smoke from her mouth. "That's nice. Go shower, Joselyn. When you come out, there will be a dress on your bed for you to wear."

"Where are we going? What are we doing?" I asked, not taking a breath. I didn't care that she hadn't wished me a happy birthday. She had bought me a dress and was taking me out.

"Just go take a shower, dammit!" she spat, causing me to jump.

I paused, glaring at her for a beat, then turned my head to look at Bryce. He was watching cartoons without a care in the world. I tried hard—really hard not to roll my eyes as I brushed past her. I was used to her yelling, but for one day—just one—I wished she would take into account that it was my birthday and act sweet.

Before I went to the bathroom to shower, I folded Bryce's picture and put it in my purse to take with me. I didn't want Mother to do something with it. I didn't trust her. I never kept anything I didn't want her *not* to throw away. Granted I didn't have much to begin with. I didn't have jewelry. I didn't have nice clothes. I didn't have CDs. I didn't have books. I didn't have DVDs. I didn't have anything except a photo of Bryce and me, one of me, Cat, and Seth from three summers ago that we took during Seth's last summer visit, and a few pictures Bryce had drawn for me at school. I kept Bryce's pictures he colored for me under my mattress and my photos in my purse.

Tonight I was going out for my birthday, and I was dressed up—something I'd never done.

When I returned to my room, there was a dress lying on my twin bed. I held it up in front of me; it barely came to my mid-thigh. It was a simple, sleeveless black dress. I didn't have a strapless bra, but I could go one night without one—depending on what we did. I didn't care. I was happy for once. It was getting to be dinner time, so hopefully we'd have a nice meal because I could go for something other than soup or a grilled cheese sandwich.

Still smiling, I slipped the dress on. Before I could slide into the sky-high, black heels my mother had placed by my bed, she came into my room without knocking. "You need to do your hair and makeup, too."

"Are you going to tell me where we're going?"

"No." There was the short, snappy answer again.

Whatever.

I went back into the bathroom and found Mother's makeup. I didn't have money to buy my own and she'd never bought me any, so I had no idea what I was doing. I didn't wear makeup. Hell, I didn't even know what she meant by I needed *to do* my hair. I covered my entire face with foundation, brushed a light beige across my eyelids, and then put on a little mascara. After I quickly dried my hair, I returned to my room.

Mother was sitting on my bed, still dressed in her robe. "You need more makeup."

"I do?"

She huffed and then stood. "Let me show you." She grabbed my wrist and tugged me behind her toward the bathroom.

"Ow! You're hurting me," I whined.

"Oh shut up, Joselyn. Stop acting like a baby."

I could feel my blood start to boil. She was such a bitch. It was my birthday. The one day that was supposed to be *your* day; a day when *you* got whatever you wanted. Before Seth became an *adult*, I'd had him and Cat to watch movies with, make me lunch, cake—*whatever.* This year Cat was off on a family vacation in Hawaii. They'd wanted one last family trip before she graduated and left for college. I wanted a first one.

Again—*whatever.*

I leaned against the olive green pedestal sink while my mother painted my face. When I turned to face the mirror, I didn't recognize myself. The freckles that lightly dusted my upper cheeks and nose were covered up completely with foundation. My eyelids were caked with pink eye shadow and black eyeliner circled each eye completely.

"Wow," I whispered.

"You look beautiful, Joss."

My gaze flicked to hers. I'd never heard her compliment me before. "Now will you tell me where we're going?"

"We're not going anywhere. *You* are."

"Huh?" Thoughts of Seth and Cat surprising me for my birthday flashed in my head, but I knew they were both out of town.

"Get your shoes on and let's go."

I didn't want to argue with her—I knew the consequences. I went to my room, slipped on the heels, grabbed my black clutch purse that had nothing in it but my pictures and lip gloss, and stumbled my way to the living room where she was waiting for me.

"There's a limo waiting for you outside," she affirmed, puffing on another cigarette. She really needed to stop that nasty shit. I was tired of smelling like stale smoke all the time.

"There's a limo waiting for me outside?" I motioned between my chest and the door.

"Yes. Now go." She urged me to take a step and I caught myself before I fell flat on my face. I wasn't used to wearing heels.

"Bye, B." I waved to Bryce as he continued to watch *101 Dalmatians.* He didn't look away or say goodbye as he recited every line.

As I stepped out of the trailer, excitement flowing through my veins. I had no idea what was going on, but finally my mother had remembered my birthday. This was going to be the best birthday ever! I turned to give her a hug. I wanted to show her how thankful I was that she'd finally remembered my birthday, but something flashed in her eyes. Instead, I stopped and only said, "Thank you." I thanked her for the dress, the limo, but most of all, I thanked her for finally remembering it was my birthday.

"No, *thank you.*" She smirked.

"What?" The humid Florida air caused my long hair to cling to my neck and chin as I whipped around to see what she meant.

"Just go, Joselyn."

When I turned toward the dirt road, there was a black limo with a man in a suit waiting outside the open door. *Fancy.* A smile spread across my face as I walked to the car. "Hi," I greeted the mystery man as he gestured to the open door. I slid into the car, the cool, black leather kissing my bare legs. A moment later, the door closed and I looked straight ahead at an unfamiliar face.

"You look just like your mother did when she was your age," he mused.

My heart stopped and my palms became clammy. "Um … okay?"

"We've met, you know." His Latino accent laced his words.

"Um, okay?"

"You were just a baby."

"Um, okay?" I had no other words. I was in a moving car with an unfamiliar man who apparently knew me—a man who my mother had sent me to.

"I'm Tony, sweetheart."

Chapter Two

Paul

Two years prior …

The bell rang, so I hurried to my locker to grab my history book for fourth period. When I opened it, a familiar piece of paper was sticking out of the top of the book and I smiled. Vanessa knew my schedule inside out. I had just kissed her during out fifteen minute break before third period, but it didn't matter; we'd sent each other notes between periods every school day since we started dating a year and a half ago.

I stuffed the note in my pocket and the book in my backpack and then hurried to my next class before I was late. I made it to class before the bell and then pulled the folded note from my pocket. It was a note that we'd been writing back and forth on the same piece of binder paper.

"You.

Me.

Lunch."

The smile that was plastered across my face wouldn't have budged even if you'd punched me as hard as you could square in the jaw. I didn't know what she meant, but whatever it was, I liked the "you and me" part. I didn't even care if I didn't eat. I'd scarf down my food in fifth period if I had to.

After class, I went back to my locker to find Vanessa leaning against it. She was talking to people as they passed and when she saw me approach, she grabbed my hand and tugged me behind her.

"Wait, sunshine. I need to put my book in my locker."

She sighed. "Hurry and grab your econ book too."

I raised an eyebrow at her. "We won't be coming back before fifth period?"

"Nope." She smiled and shook her head.

I eyed her curiously. "You have me intrigued."

She lifted up on her tiptoes and whispered in my ear, "And you have me horny."

I was tearing my backpack opened so fast I thought for sure the zipper would break, but it didn't. I threw my history book in my locker, switched it out with my econ book, and slammed the metal door shut with enough force to cause every girl within a twenty-foot radius to jump and the dudes to turn and look at us. From an outsider's perspective, you might think we were fighting, I was only excited about getting a nooner and tempted to shout the news down the hall.

Vanessa giggled as I grabbed her hand and led her to my car so I could drive us to a nearby park for *lunch.*

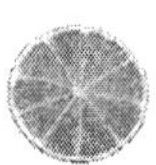

Game day.

One of my favorite days.

I loved the rush I got from the energy of the crowd as I drove the football into the end zone. We all had our passions and football was mine. I practiced every day and I stayed focused because I had my future all mapped out—my future with Vanessa.

We sat on the grass under a tree with the rest of our group of friends during lunch. Today there would be no nooner and I couldn't skip eating because I had to make sure I was fueled up and ready for tonight.

She sat between my legs, leaning against my chest and wearing my teal and black Letterman jacket to stay warm. "Tomorrow after practice do you want to see a movie?" she asked, looking up at me.

I tilted my head down a little and kissed her forehead. "Yeah, sunshine, whatever you want to do."

"What if we go check out some of the apartments next to UCLA and see what they're like?"

"Oh, so now you want to live with me?" I teased. After we graduated, I was going to go to the University of California Los Angeles and Vanessa would get into modeling. She'd already modeled for a few catalogs and had been featured in an orange juice commercial when she was younger, but she wanted to be the next Cindy Crawford and I knew she could be.

She sat up, then turned around on her knees and grabbed my

cheeks with both her hands playfully. Our mouths were inches apart as she looked directly into my eyes. "Wouldn't it be better if we lived together, rather than you being tired all the time in class?"

I cracked a smile. "And why would I be tired all the time?"

"Oh my God, if you two don't go get a room—"

"Shh, Amber, Nessa is telling me something important. Go on," I promoted.

"You know you can't get enough of me," she whispered. "So if we aren't living together," I let her continue, but I knew what she would say because we'd already had a similar conversation. We were in love and I wanted to live with her. I didn't care about living on campus. I wanted to be with *her.* I could still go to parties, still hang with friends, hang with teammates. We could find an apartment close to campus. "You'll be sleeping less because you'll have to commute all the time."

"I like where your head is at, and I like what you're thinking right *now.*"

She smirked. "How do you know what I'm thinking?"

"Please, sunshine. I know everything about you." I kissed her lips briefly.

"Seriously, get a room," Amber groaned.

"We can find a place close to campus. It won't be bad. Trust me."

She smiled before she agreed and then kissed me quickly and turned back around in my arms. We stayed like that the rest of our lunch break while the group chatted about the game and weekend plans. When the bell rang, Vanessa handed me a folded up piece of paper.

"Can't wait to see you kick ass tonight! Maybe after, I'll let you smack mine."

A million thoughts ran through my head. Okay two: doggie or anal. I was down for either.

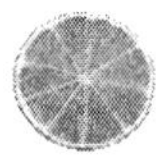

The Friday night lights shined down on the brown leather pigskin between my gloved fingers as I ran, dodging the blur of white and missing the body that tried to tackle me as I made my way toward the end zone. With each stride, I breathed in the cool sea breeze coming from the Pacific Ocean just a little over a block away.

I dodged another tackle before meeting the safety head on at the goal line. Our helmets clashed together, vibrating against my skull and causing me to lose focus for a slight second. I powered through, spinning and falling over the white line to make another touchdown. The crowd went wild, the cheers deafening, but there was just one I cared about. After I stood and tossed the football to the referee, I scanned the bleachers for my girl.

The moment my eyes locked with hers, it confirmed something was wrong. I'd noticed something was off every time I'd looked at her during the game. She wasn't cheering, she wasn't laughing with Amber, and she wasn't bright like the sun—my sunshine. Vanessa was only clapping with the crowd and giving me a tight smile. Something was definitely wrong and I didn't like it.

What the fuck?

I wanted to run up and ask, but I couldn't. We were in the fourth quarter with only four minutes left. I would get answers soon enough, though. Every Friday night after our home games, we went across the street to the beach to celebrate all *my* touchdowns.

Tonight would be no different.

After all, I had three to celebrate—so far.

"PJ!" Marcus yelled, slapping me on the back. "Nice game."

I gave him a nod as I scanned the crowd of bodies, searching for my girl. Most home games were the same: we won, and then the school came across the street to celebrate with a bonfire. We would have a few kegs in the back of trucks that were easy to drive off with if the cops showed up, and we'd all drink until we couldn't feel the cold California breeze any longer. A few would light up or smoke weed, but I wasn't into that shit. I was more or less a superstar for Malibu High; an athlete with a full ride to UCLA and graduating this year. I couldn't chance anything happening.

My gaze continued to scan the crowd as best I could in the dark, the only light coming from the orange flame of the fire burning and the moon. I didn't see Vanessa or Amber anywhere.

"Bro, that was sick at the end how you just plowed through that dude for your fourth TD of the night," Clint, another classmate, beamed, reaching out his hand to bring me in for a bro-hug.

"Thanks, man." I smiled. "Have you seen Nessa?"

"Yeah, I think I saw her go down to the water."

"Cool." I clapped him on the back and started to jog around the people and through the sand until I got in the clear. I looked right and then left, but didn't spot her. I was about to turn around and go back when, out of the corner of my eye, I saw her and Amber sitting on a rock to my left, not near the water at all. I jogged over to them.

"Hey, sunshine, you okay?" I asked, kneeling down so I was eye to eye with her.

She looked to Amber before turning toward me. "We need to talk."

"Do you want me to stay?" Amber asked.

Why the fuck would Amber need to stay for me to talk to my girlfriend?

Vanessa shook her head. "No, I'll be okay."

"What's going on?" I asked as Amber walked away. Vanessa looked to her right and then back to me, her glassy brown eyes looking into mine.

"What's wrong?" I sat on the rock and pulled Vanessa into my lap, draping her legs over mine. She rested her head on my shoulder, her left arm around my neck as she started to cry.

"Talk to me, babe."

She sniffled. "I'm …" She stopped and I waited, but she only cried more. I pulled her as close to me as I could. She was almost shivering in my Letterman jacket.

"What's wrong, sunshine? Is it us?" She stilled and my heart sank. "Sun—"

"I'm pregnant!" she blurted.

She cried harder, her body shaking in my arms, and I rocked her until she stopped crying because I had no idea what else to do. As I sat with her in my arms, staring out into the dark sky with the ocean waves crashing in the distance, the thought hit me.

I was going to be a father at eighteen.

We stared at the pregnancy tests, both not sure if we were reading them correctly. We decided she should take five more home tests to make sure she was really pregnant.

"Does one or two lines mean that you're pregnant?" I asked her. She stared at the sticks, not saying anything. "Sunshine…"

"I'm pregnant."

"No." I shook my head. "I pull out each time."

"Fuck, Paul, this can't be happening. We can't be parents. I'm going to be a supermodel. I can't have stretch marks."

"They have Photoshop," I joked, trying to make light of the situation. I was freaking out, but I didn't want to show it because if I did then she'd freak out more and I didn't want my parents to hear.

"Are you serious right now?" she snapped.

"Yes, I'm serious. No model is one-hundred percent natural on anything out there."

"I can't have a baby, Paul!"

I didn't like when she used my real name. People called me PJ and when things got hot and heavy, Vanessa called me God. "We'll make it work. I promise." I'd commute to UCLA from Malibu, and while she went to shoots, our parents could take care of the baby when I was in class or had a game. We could make this work. I knew we could. We were both staying local.

She started pacing my room. "How can we make it work? I don't want a kid, Paul. *I* have dreams."

"And *I* don't?" Her tone made me snap.

"Of course you do, but mine are about my looks. I can't be some fat heifer with stretch marks."

I watched her pace for a moment. "Do you care about my dreams?"

She stopped walking and tilted her head slightly as if I'd lost my mind. "Of course I do."

My heart was hurting the more she talked only about *her* dreams. We always talked about *our* dreams; how I would go pro, how she would be a supermodel, how we would get married, how we would start a family, and how we would be together forever. I knew we didn't plan to get pregnant during high school, but Vanessa didn't have plans to attend college like I had. Did she even think about that? Did she even care?

"Do you?" I challenged. "Because I'm willing to bust my ass every day to build a future for *us*, Vanessa. Not *me*. *Us*!" I snapped. "Do you even love me?"

Her head snapped back as if I'd slapped her. "What?"

"I'm starting to get the feeling that you don't."

"How could you say that?"

I expected her to cry. Part of me had said it to see if she would. Maybe I was an asshole because I *wanted* her to cry, to prove she cared about me and not the stretch marks she'd get from being pregnant—

that she'd kept mentioning.

"Well, do you?"

She hesitated before answering and at that moment I had my answer. "Yes, of—"

I chuckled sarcastically. "You're just with me because I'm the captain of the football team. Fucking All-State tight end. You think going along with me is going to get you places, sugar?"

"Why are you saying these things to me?" she whispered.

"They're true aren't they? Tell me, Vanessa, what are you more upset about? Being pregnant because of stretch marks or having a baby at seventeen?" I didn't bother to ask if having a baby with me was a factor. If she was tied to me for eighteen years and I was a pro-football player, then she'd at least get money out of me and that had probably been her plan all along.

"I'm gonna go."

"You do that," I hissed. I was done. I needed to cool off before I said something more I'd regret. Vanessa had my entire heart, but the more I spoke, the more I felt myself pushing her away.

When she opened the door to my room, she turned. "The real reason I was crying last night wasn't because I'm pregnant. It's because I never thought I'd have to go through an abortion."

My head snapped up. "You've already made up your mind?"

"Of course I have. I'm seventeen, PJ. I can't be tied down with a baby. *I* have dreams."

I pulled her back into my room and shut the door. "What do you mean you've already made up your mind?" I barked, spit flying from my mouth.

She wiped her chin. "You don't get to make this decision."

"The hell I don't!"

"It's my body!"

I stepped closer, coming nose to nose with her. "It's my baby, too. My fucking blood."

"This is not up for discussion anymore." She pushed my chest, but I didn't budge. I was like a brick wall especially when I was pissed as fuck. "Move out of my way."

"No." I shook my head.

She started to poke my chest with each word. "I. Don't. Want. Kids. Now get out of my way!"

I stared at her. "You're going to get rid of our baby? It's a part of us! We made that baby together and you're just going to go and get rid of it? You really don't love me, do you?" She looked past me, not saying a word.

I had my answer.

"You disgust me. Get the fuck out of here," I spat. I didn't know what more to say or do. She was carrying my baby and was going to get rid of it like it was yesterday's trash. She didn't once shed a tear. I, however, cried like a little bitch the moment I saw her pull away.

She was taking more than just my heart with her; she was taking something I'd created. I was by no means ready to be a father, but I wanted to be with Vanessa forever. I loved her more than anything … More than football. She was the first thing I thought about when I woke up in the morning and the last thing I thought about when I went to sleep at night.

And now we were done.

After I'd manned up, I got in my car and drove around for an hour feeling weak until I saw a sign:

Army Strong

It was as if it was calling to me. Without another thought, I pulled in front of the building, turned off my car, and walked inside.

That was the day I put my country's dreams before my own.

Chapter Three

Joselyn

Two years later …

H*oly fuck*. "Um, okay?"

He chuckled. "You have no idea do you?"

"What do you mean?"

"So you *do* know more than two words?" I rolled my eyes. Crossing my arms over my chest, I looked out the heavy tinted window at the passing street lights. "I wouldn't give me attitude, sweetheart. You don't know what I'm capable of."

I turned and straightened my head back toward him. "What am I doing here?"

He smiled. "You have a date."

"With …" I paused and then took a big swallow of nothing before I was able to speak again. "With you?"

He gave a deep belly laugh and then leaned forward to grab the champagne bottle that was sitting in a bucket of ice. "As much as I would love to get a taste of your pure pussy … It is pure right?" He gestured with the bottle toward me. I curled up my lips in disgust and grunted. "I'll take that as a yes." He laughed. "Whales pay a lot of money to fuck a virgin."

"Wait. What?" I sat up straighter, trying to sit as far back as I could from this man. I felt cornered, trapped and my heart began to race so fast that I knew if I didn't calm the fuck down, I was going to pass out.

He filled two flutes then leaned forward, his arm reaching out with one of the champagne flutes in his hand. I glanced at the bubbly liquid and then back up to his face, finally getting a good look at the man sitting across from me. The interior of the limo was dark, the only light from the pin-point, multi-colored lights on the ceiling shining down, but I could see the skin on his face was a deep sun-kissed brown. Tony had dark eyes and a neatly trimmed goatee that was the same color as the hair on his head.

I'd never had a sip of alcohol before because I'd never had the desire to try it. I'd seen Mother come home drunk too many times and I never wanted to be like her. But at this moment not being in *this* moment sounded like the best idea. I couldn't believe what was happening and on my birthday of all days. I reached for the glass with a shaky hand, my gaze dropping down to the massive gold ring on the ring finger of his right hand and then took a sip—a big one of the bubbly liquid. It was tart and didn't taste that great. I'd expected it to taste like juice. *Why did people drink this shit?*

"This is how it's going to go, sweetheart." He took a sip of his champagne as he leaned back in his seat. The colored lights from the ceiling shined down on his white shirt under his black suit jacket and I stared at them and not his face. "We're driving to a hotel where your date Marco will be waiting for you. Jose will bring you up to Marco's room, and then you'll do *whatever* Marco wants you to do for two hours. Jose will drive you home when you're done."

"Who's Jose?" *Like that was the most important question to ask.*

"The limo driver."

"And where will you be?"

"I don't make a habit of escorting my girls to meet their johns."

"Um, what?"

"Which part didn't you understand because we're almost at the hotel?"

"I'm working for you?"

"Isn't it obvious?"

"I can't work for you. I'm seventeen. I'm in high school. And my best friend is a cop!"

He laughed and rubbed his goatee with his thumb and index finger. "Sweetheart, please, I have cops on my payroll. They don't scare me. And your mother started much younger than you and look how she turned out."

Exactly.

"You don't have *this* cop on your payroll."

He leaned forward as the car pulled to a stop. Tony pushed a button, telling Jose to give us just another minute, and then turned his attention back to me. "If I hear from Marco that you were not cooperative in *every* way, you and your mother are going to pay." I blinked at him. "Do I make myself clear?"

"I thought you cared about my mother?"

He gave another laugh, the same one I knew would give me nightmares. "Sweetheart, your mother is nothing more than a whore makin' me a shit load of money."

"A whore?" I spat. "You turned her into one!"

He grinned. "It's what I'm good at."

Before I could respond further, the door opened and a hand reached inside. I looked up, then back at Tony and he nodded. This couldn't be happening. This was supposed to be my surprise birthday dinner. Instead, I was about to walk into a hotel and lose my virginity.

"Go on, sweetheart."

A lump was forming in my throat and tears were on the verge of spilling over my eyelids, but instead, I put my big girl panties on and grabbed Jose's hand as he helped me out of the limo. My heart was beating so hard I thought it was going to beat out my chest and onto the stone walkway as I took a few steps on wobbly legs until I got my balance in the ridiculously high heels. Now I understood the makeup, the dress, and the shoes. And to think I had thanked my mother for this.

Jose and I walked side by side through the sliding glass doors and into the lobby of the hotel. A bellman or a valet (I wasn't sure which) greeted us with a tip of his head and I wondered if he thought we were together. Jose was old enough to be my father. Tony was old enough to be my father and I was willing to bet Marco was old enough to be my father.

I thought about coming up with an excuse to use the phone to call Seth when I got up to the hotel room, but I didn't know his phone number. I'd left it in my room under my mattress where Mother wouldn't find it. I needed him—he made me feel safe. Could I call the D.C. Police Department and ask for Officer McKenna? Did it work that way? When I watched police shows, they had different precincts—was that how the real world worked? Every thought was running through my head at a million miles an hour.

As we stepped up to a wall of elevators, everything around me disappeared. I wanted to make a break for it, run through the lobby, run out the doors and run for my life, but I was in these damn heels and by the time I kicked them off, Jose was bound to catch me. I didn't look at the button Jose had pushed. I didn't remember getting on the elevator. Everything was a daze and I didn't want to register that *this* was really happening.

Finally, the elevator stopped and Jose gestured for me to exit. I stepped out, but he didn't follow. I turned slightly, wondering why he didn't move. "In two hours, I'll meet you here, Miss Marquez."

"Two hours," I confirmed, barely audible.

"You better go or you'll be late. If you're late, then your pay gets docked."

"My pay?" I questioned.

"Si," he answered. "If you don't show up on time, Tony will find out. You don't want to disappoint Tony, yes?"

I nodded. "Yes." I figured I shouldn't question Jose. Like me, he was only an employee. Fuck—I was an employee. How did that happen? Oh right, my mother.

"If I hear from Marco that you were not cooperative in every way, you and your

mother are going to pay."

I gave Jose a tight smile and took the steps down the hallway to the single door. I could hear my heart beating in my ears and it took everything in me not to break down and cry. Instead, I took a deep breath and raised my right hand, knocking lightly. A moment later I was staring into the eyes of the man who had *bought* me for two hours.

"Bella. Please, come in."

Bella? Really? I wanted to roll my eyes and tell him my name wasn't Bella, but instead, I smiled a shy smile and entered, stepping around him as he closed the door behind him. The hairs on the back of my neck prickled and I was certain it wasn't from the air-conditioning in the massive suite I'd just entered. Before I could get a good look at the space, Marco spoke, coming around me so we were face-to-face.

"Do you prefer red or white?" I scrunched my eyebrows at him. He laughed. "Wine. Do you prefer red or white wine?"

Maybe he didn't know I was underage? Maybe this was how hookers got through the night? Hell if I knew. "I'm not sure. I guess white." I shrugged. I assumed white since I'd just had white champagne in the limo. I didn't even like that shit, but if I had to get tipsy to get through the next two hours, I was going to chug whatever I needed to.

As Marco uncorked and poured the wine, I stared at him. I wanted to get a good look at the man who was willing to pay a large amount of money to fuck a virgin. Marco wasn't bad on the eyes. In fact, he was easy on them as I'd heard people say. He had a lightly trimmed beard that was more stubble than anything, brown hair that was spiked perfectly with specks of grey on the sides, and when he smiled as he laughed, the creases accented his cheeks as if they were dimples—but they weren't. The lines traveled down to a straight jaw that was strong and manly. The thought of his age was enough to make me want to throw up in my mouth. Instead, I reached out and grabbed the glass of wine as he handed it to me.

"You want to hold it by the stem so the wine doesn't warm from your body heat."

"Oh … okay." I slid my hand down to the stem.

"Let me take your purse."

"I'll just set it by the door and take my heels off—"

"No, bella. You leave your heels on."

On my way to the entry table, I took big gulps of the sour wine. I still didn't understand why adults drank such nasty shit. I was used to Kool-Aid since it was all we could afford. Wine and champagne tasted nothing like grape flavored Kool-Aid.

"You like?" Marco asked when I turned around after placing my purse on the glass top table. I looked down at the nearly empty glass. I didn't need to hold it by the stem after all. I gave a tight smile and nodded.

There was a slight squeak from the cork as he removed it from the wine bottle and I handed him my glass. My head was starting to feel light as I had to focus a few times on the liquid coming out of the bottle. He handed me the glass and I grabbed it, holding the stem between fingers and that was when we touched for the first time. I wanted to jump back, run from the room and into the elevator—

Right. The elevator.

He was bound to catch me. Instead, I smiled at him and he smiled back. "You have a lovely smile, bella."

I blushed at his compliment, even if it was coming from someone who'd paid to take my virginity. I wasn't used to getting them. "Thank you," I responded.

"Come. Let's go into the bedroom and get comfortable."

It sounded as if he did this sort of thing all the time. *Maybe he did.* Did he only do it with girls my age? Maybe some girls needed money for college and sold their virginity themselves. Maybe there were strippers who wanted to make extra money. Or maybe there were other girls like me who had no idea they were being sold until it was too late.

My legs felt heavy as I took each step, but I continued to take big gulps of the wine despite its taste. The more I drank, the more my nerves were starting to calm down. I started to slip my shoes off again, but Marco *tsked.*

"No, bella, you leave your heels on."

"The entire time?"

He smiled and I wanted so badly to like his smile, but everything was wrong about this night. "Yes."

I took another big gulp of my wine until there wasn't anymore. He reached his hand out for the glass and I handed it to him, expecting him to refill it, but instead he placed it on the desk behind him and then twirled his finger as if he wanted me to turn around. I did.

"Tony always sends me the most beautiful girls. He knows which ones are my *type.*" I felt him come up behind me and I held my breath.

"Your dark brown hair is the perfect length to wrap around my fist while I fuck you from behind."

I swallowed. "Um, what?"

I heard a slight chuckle. "They always think their first time is going to be slow and sweet, that I'll wine and dine them. You had your wine, bella, but once you're sweet, tight pussy is wrapped around me, it's not going to be slow or sweet."

I listened to the sound of running water as a single tear fell from the corner of my eye, but I couldn't let Marco see. The clock on the nightstand told me that there was still thirty minutes left of my *date*.

The haze from the alcohol had worn off, and between my legs ached, but I was happy and thankful it was over—at least I thought it was. Marco hadn't given me further instructions before he'd left to shower, but he had been in there for at least two minutes. I thought he'd come back for me, insist I take one with him. He hadn't. I glanced at the clock one more time and then toward the bathroom when I noticed his wallet on the nightstand next to the bed. Immediately a million thoughts cross my mind.

There was only one I acted on, though.

I jumped from the bed, noticing the blood between my legs as I slipped on my panties, managing to get them caught a few times on my heels. After I'd finally got the cotton bikini panties righted, I pulled my dress on, barely able to zip the back, but I didn't care. I wasn't sure how much time I had and I didn't know if Jose would be at the elevators early waiting for me.

When I opened Marco's wallet, I noticed a few credit cards, but if Tony had cops on his payroll, then they'd track me down. I'd seen it happen on television. Bypassing the cards, I opened the wallet further and pulled several bills from the inside before I grabbed my purse and opened the front door.

The shower was still running as I made a dash for the metal doors. Thankfully, Jose wasn't standing by the elevator. I pushed the down button repeatedly, praying that they would open, but before they did, I made a last minute decision to use the stairs instead.

When I opened the stairwell door, I remembered that I was on the twenty-seventh floor. My heart was pounding and the ache between my legs was unbearable, but there was no time for me to think about what had just happened in the hotel room. I needed to get out of the hotel before Marco, Jose, or even Tony saw me. I didn't know what my plan was, but I had a wad of cash and no desire to go back home to the woman who sold her daughter.

After three flights of stairs, I slipped off my heels and ran the rest of the way as fast as possible. By the time I'd reached the bottom, I was out of breath and my adrenaline was through the roof. I didn't see or hear anyone following me as I gave one last look up the stairwell before I exited and burst into the humid Miami night.

The door emptied on the side of the hotel and instead of going to the front where I assumed Jose had the limo parked, I ran the opposite way toward the back. My lungs were on fire, my hair was sticking to my neck, and rocks were digging into the soles of my feet, but I kept running. This was life or death to me.

". . . you and your mother are going to pay."

She deserved to pay after she'd sold her own daughter to be a whore, but I would miss Bryce. My eyes began to sting at the thought of never seeing him again, but there was no way I could go back for him. Mrs. McKenna would take care of him if something happened to Mother, I was certain of it. But right now, I needed to save myself and get the hell out of here.

As I approached the street, a taxi was coming and I flagged it down. It stopped and I jumped in.

"Where to?" the driver asked.

I had no idea. I just needed to get away from the hotel. I thought for a moment. "Um … Is there a bus or a train station nearby?"

"There's a Greyhound station," he replied in an Armenian accent, "but it's not that close."

I met his gaze in the rearview mirror. "That's perfect. Thank you."

"The fare will cost you."

"That's okay."

"You sure?"

"Yes, I'm sure."

Chapter Four

Paul

Twelve years later …

Present Day

Helping my best friend plan his proposal felt as though someone had a death grip on my heart and wouldn't let go.

For the last ten or so years, I hadn't been able to think about spending the rest of my life with only one woman. After Vanessa, I didn't want to be tied down. I wanted as much pussy as I could get. And I *was* getting it. Now helping Gabe pick out the ring for Autumn and coming up with the proposal brought back memories of *her* and how you're *supposed* to marry your first love. At least that's what I'd thought.

They say things happen for a reason …

Cochran, Gabe's first love, had died in his arms while we were in Afghanistan on a MEDEVAC call. Autumn was perfect for him, though—maybe more so than Cochran. But, of course, I'd never tell him that.

The house was silent as I woke and made my way to the kitchen for my morning cup of coffee and breakfast. I looked into Gabe and Autumn's bare room as I passed. It was weird being without roommates after so long. Gabe and I had started rooming together when we moved to Vegas from Malibu. Autumn moved in not long after, but I wouldn't have had it any other way. Her husband, who was our Major from the Army, hadn't taken it too well when he'd learned that Autumn was leaving him, but Gabe and I hadn't taken it too well when we'd learned that he was putting his hands on her. Major Dick got what was coming to him when he was poisoned by a business associate.

Even in the Army I'd had someone to harass in the morning. Okay not harass, but I liked making breakfast for more than just me even if it were for grouchy ass Gabe. But now Gabe and Autumn were engaged and had their own house, and I had a house all to myself.

I didn't like it.

I needed a dog or something.

Turning from the empty room, I walked to the kitchen and made my coffee. I ate breakfast quickly, then dressed and headed for Club 24 where the three of us worked out. We also taught self-defense classes there until we could save enough money to open our own location. Gabe and I naturally wanted to protect people since our time in the Army, and after everything that had happened in Autumn's past with her husband, it was only fitting to get certified to teach self-defense classes and to teach people how to shoot. Our company taught both types of classes. One was at Club 24 and the other was out on the range.

Before heading out the door, I grabbed a bottle of champagne and a few plastic cups. We had celebrating to do. Two of my favorite people were getting married—as long as Gabe didn't fuck up the proposal.

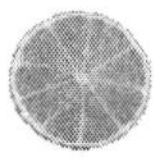

Club 24 had *everything* you needed to meet your fitness goals. Aside from your standard treadmills, elliptical machines, stationary bikes and weightlifting equipment you'd find at any gym, they offered yoga, Zumba, kickboxing, Kenpo, self-defense classes (with yours truly), cycling, aerobics, indoor volleyball, beach volleyball, and racquetball.

"Should we pop this now or after class?" I held the bottle of champagne up with my left hand and walked through the steel door where our class was being held in a half an hour. Autumn unwrapped her arms from around Gabe's neck and turned toward me.

"You want to drink *before* class?"

"It's only champagne. Like a mimosa without the OJ, Auttie." I winked. "I see you said yes, by the way." I motioned with my head at her left hand and greeted Gabe with a head nod.

Gabe shook his head and walked over to the sound system. "No one's drinking before class."

"Cap—" He was my captain for so long that it still slipped, especially when he ordered me around. "Fine. After class, but then we're drinking more than this cheap ass champagne I found at home." Gabe liked his whiskey. I liked tequila, especially a shot of it after I'd licked salt off the skin of a chick, followed by a slurp of lime juice from her navel.

They both shared an odd look without saying anything. "What?" I asked. They shared another look. "Jesus. What?" I asked again.

Autumn turned to me. "I haven't been to the doctor yet, but ..." She paused and they shared another silent look. "I'm pregnant," she finally blurted.

I blinked. Then tore my gaze from Autumn to Gabe to check for his reaction. I wasn't sure if I should be happy for him. I knew he was in love with Autumn, but I also knew this was a new relationship and I knew how much he'd loved Cochran. What I saw when I looked into Gabe's eyes made me smile.

It wasn't what I saw when we were in Afghanistan and he'd snuck around with Cochran.

It wasn't what I saw when we'd first moved to Vegas and he wanted to find out who Autumn was.

It wasn't what I saw when we were at Autumn's house and had to fight off her husband to protect her.

It wasn't what I saw when he thought she left him when she learned what he did for a living and *it wasn't* what I saw when he was nervous because he thought she might say no when he was going to propose.

What I saw was a man's life finally going the way it was meant to go. The look on his face was pure adoration and he was smiling with a twinkle in his eye.

"Holy fucking shit, dude!" I reached for both of them and engulfed them the best I could in a group hug. "All that fucking I heard you guys doing—no wonder you got knocked up."

Autumn tried to push off of me, but I kept her from budging. "I'm going to pretend you didn't just say that," she mumbled into my side.

Gabe broke free from my grasp. "What did I tell you about letting her know you could hear?"

"You knew?" she asked.

I laughed and set my gym bag and the champagne down in the cabinet while they spoke. Gabe whispered mumbled, but I could still hear him. "Did you really think he couldn't hear you when you came, angel?"

She whispered back, stepping closer. I pretended to get items to set up for class, but really I was enjoying the show. I was going to miss living with them. "Every time?" she asked.

He chuckled. "Every time, but especially when you'd squirt."

The throwing dummy I was carrying in my hands slipped from my grasp and they both turned and looked at me. I smiled and Autumn groaned, shoving Gabe a little before turning toward the door to leave. "I… I'll be back," she muttered, throwing her hands in the air before she left.

"Really, dude?" Gabe asked.

"You're mad at me?"

"You're buying all my drinks."

"Whatever." I laughed. "You know you're not mad. You used to fuck for a living."

"Yeah, but remember that Autumn's still sensitive about the situation even if it is my *fucking* skills."

"All right, enough about your fucking skills. Let's go get a drink. I'll buy since you insist." I slugged him on the arm and then turned and grabbed the rest of the dummies for class.

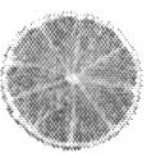

Autumn couldn't look me in the eye the entire class.

It wasn't as though I had walked in on her butt ass naked. And really, she knew what I did for a living aside from our business. If a chick wasn't screaming, we weren't doin' it right.

"Blue Martini or what?" I asked as we cleaned up the mats.

"I'm gonna go to Brandi's," Autumn stated. She kissed Gabe.

"Have fun, angel."

I watched as she left, still not looking at me. "Bye, Auttie!" I shouted and laughed. "Nice of her to help us put this shit away."

"Bro code, dude. Bro code."

"Fuck. I got it. Let's drop it. This isn't my fault."

"Let's go get that drink then."

I groaned. "Actually, let's go back to the house and have some beers. Help me move my shit into your old room. I have a feeling Mark's gonna find me a new roommate soon and that fucker's not getting the master."

"You're lucky you're my best friend."

"Yeah, yeah. Let's do this shit. I have work tonight."

I worked as a male escort for a company called Saddles & Racks, but I didn't get paid for sex. I got paid for my time and companionship. I get paid to make ladies feel wanted; to feel as though they were the only woman in the room.

My date for the evening was the typical drinks followed by *whatever* we wanted to do for the two hours she was paying for. I'd been on quite a few dates in the past five years, so it was almost second nature. I didn't hook up with a chick on every date; some didn't want that. Some wanted a date for an event. Some wanted to make someone jealous. Some wanted a date for an entire weekend. Hell, some wanted a date for an entire month. I hadn't found that client yet, but my buddy Nick had. And, of course, there were those dates who wanted a good fucking. I needed to be attracted to them, though. I had to be able to get it up *if you know what I mean.*

When I arrived at Gold Spike in downtown Vegas, I scanned the dimly lit room. I'd never heard of Gold Spike before and when I entered, I immediately couldn't wait to return with Gabe. They had pool, cornhole, shuffleboard, and lounge areas to sit and chat. I couldn't believe I hadn't heard about this place before. Granted, I hadn't been in Vegas for very long, but damn, this was right up my alley. Drinks plus competitive gaming? Sold!

The instructions for my date were that Nancy wanted me to notice her from across the room. She was going to be with a group of her friends for drinks. She told Mark (my boss) that it was because she was the heaviest one of her friends and usually the guys always bought drinks for them and not her. She always felt like the ugly one.

What most guys didn't realize was that a smile was the most beautiful thing on a woman's body. If they made a woman smile, her eyes would light up and then everything would start to glow.

I spotted Nancy instantly. I hadn't seen a picture, but her lack of confidence wasn't hard to spot. She wasn't smiling as wide as the others, and she wasn't laughing as loud either. She sat at the far end of the room, sipping her drink, and her leg bouncing up and down under the table.

As I made my way to the bar, I briefly made eye contact with her. Her eyes grew big as her gaze met mine and then she quickly looked down at the table. I chuckled and continued to the bar. It was normal for these types of dates to be nervous. My regulars, on the other hand, knew what they wanted.

I sat on a stool and ordered a beer, frequently making eye contact with Nancy through the mirror that ran along a side wall. A few times I caught her gaze and the more it happened, the longer she kept hers on mine. For this to work, I needed her to be comfortable. I knew this was out of the ordinary for her, but when I walked up to her after she accepted my drink from the bartender, I needed her to actually talk to me. After motioning for the bartender, I instructed him to send her whatever she was drinking. He nodded and turned.

Then, I waited.

This was the moment Nancy was waiting for and one of the reasons I loved my job. I was dying to see the look on her friend's faces when she was the one who got the drink. All eyes would be on me in … three … two … one …

"Oh my God."

"Who?"

"Where?"

"Him?"

"Holy shit!"

"Fuck me!"

"He's hot."

"Shhh, you're being too loud!"

Women were conspicuous even when they thought they weren't. I laughed around a pull of my beer as I looked at Nancy. She wasn't looking back, but she did look like maybe she was trying to explain to her friends how someone like me could want someone like her. *She needs better friends.*

I finished my beer in two gulps, set it down and stood. Time was ticking on the two hours she'd paid for and her friends needed to be out of the picture. As I walked the good fifteen feet to where they were sitting at a long, counter-high table, I heard hushed whispers and then silence as I stopped by Nancy's side.

She was sitting on the far end and looked up at me through the curtain of her light brown bangs, her hand playing with the straw of her drink nervously. I could feel all five sets of eyes on me, waiting for me to speak. If I were any Joe Schmo, I'd probably be nervous walking into the lion's den, but instead I smiled and nodded hello.

"Ladies," I greeted.

"Hi," they said in unison.

I turned my attention to Nancy. "I've had a pretty shitty day, but I saw you from across the bar and the way you were smiling and laughing caught my eye. I was wondering if you'd like to finish your drink with me?"

Nancy's eyes became huge again. I wasn't sure why. She knew this was coming. Her face was a little flush too. Maybe she'd thought that Saddles & Racks was too good to be true. You'd get what you paid for; especially when it came to me.

"Don't leave the man hanging, Nance," one of the friends remarked.

"I'd… I'd love to," she finally agreed and began to stand, but I reached out my hand and helped her up. She reached down and took her glass while she smiled at her friends. It was the first real smile I'd seen from her since I'd been at Gold Spike. After I'd stopped at the bar to order myself another beer, I led her to a corner table on the opposite side of the bar where I was before so we could have privacy to talk.

"That was perfect," she breathed, her smile still as wide as it was when we'd left her friends.

"Those are three words I don't get tired of hearing," I joked. She let out a loud laugh and I looked toward the table where her friends were sitting. Sure enough, they were all looking at us. "Do you ever get the feeling you're being watched?"

She stopped laughing. "Not usually."

I reached up and grabbed the end of her shoulder-length, curly brown hair. "Why do you think your friends get more attention?"

"Just look at them." She waved a hand in their direction.

"Are you referring to their looks?"

"Well… yeah."

"Sugar, I've known some beautiful women with shitty personalities that make them the ugliest bitches around. It's not what's on the outside that matters."

"But you wouldn't have bought me this drink if I wasn't paying you."

"Well, I wouldn't have been here tonight to buy you the drink, so that's true. But when I walked in here looking for you, I knew who you were because you lacked what the others had. You need to have that spark. You're beautiful. Who cares if you're not a size zero. Really, my dick would break you if you were a size zero."

Her eyes widened and I chuckled. It had been awhile since I'd had a date who was this shy. Usually, my dates wanted a good, hard fucking—if it got to that stage. It had to be natural as if we really felt the attraction between the two of us.

She swallowed hard, then took a sip of her drink. "So… um, how did you become an escort anyway?"

Well, we had another hour to spare. I could kill it by telling her the story. "I'd just gotten out of the Army and moved back to Malibu. I had no idea what I wanted to do, and the last time I'd been home was when I graduated high school."

"Wow, you've been an escort for a long time then."

I smiled. "Not that long. When we had leave, I never went home because there was someone I didn't want to see and I figured I'd run into her."

"Oh, an ex-girlfriend."

"Right." I nodded.

"But the Los Angeles area is huge."

"L.A. is huge, but Malibu is small and so was the group of people we hung out with."

"So she stuck around after high school."

"Exactly. She thought she was going to get discovered by some top modeling agency and make it big, but she never did."

"Is she still there?"

"Actually, no. She moved to New York to try her luck out there." I took a pull of my beer. "After my last deployment I moved back home for good. The night I heard she moved to New York was the night I knew we were officially never going to get back together. I was at a bar drowning my sorrows and I met a lady…"

"Hey, handsome."

I turned at the sound of the female's voice and watched as she ran her fake red acrylic nails along my forearm. I knew what it looked like. I was in a bar, drowning my sorrows with shots of tequila, but I wasn't looking to get laid tonight. Even though it had been almost nine years since I'd seen Vanessa, I couldn't be in this town and not think of her. I only wanted to spend my last few bucks on as much alcohol as I could.

When Cochran died, Gabe had to fight his own demons, but Vanessa was living. She didn't want me, yet I was the idiot who couldn't stop wanting her. So in front of Gabe—in front of everyone, I pretended I didn't want anyone, that I was sowing my oats. Maybe I was, but being back home was a reminder of what I'd once had. The bottle of Patrón would be my friend for the night, not this chick.

"Do you know the best way to drink a shot of tequila?" she continued. I finally

looked over at her as she sat next to me. I did know the best way—everyone knew. I cracked a smile because I couldn't help it.

"Off a woman."

She shook her head no. "Not off any woman. Off of me."

I laughed. "Off of you?"

"Yep."

"Is that so?"

"Yep, but first—"

"Get out of here, Candy."

Her eyes became huge. Without a word, she huffed and left. I turned and stood. "What the fuck?" I didn't want Candy, but seriously, what if I'd wanted to fuck her brains out until I couldn't remember my own name? It wasn't as if I was coming back to this dump again. I wasn't even in Malibu. I'd driven down the Pacific Coast until I knew I wouldn't see anyone familiar before I stopped to get my drink on.

"Listen, kid. If you want the herp, then you can fuck Candy, but I'm gonna go out on a limb and say that's not your thing." His gaze flicked down to the dog tags on my chest. "And at fifty bucks, she's a cheap hooker too."

I blinked.

He laughed. "Do you have fifty bucks?"

I shook my head. I didn't. I was spending my last few dollars on my drinks. Sure the Army was giving me money, but it wasn't enough.

"Would you like a job?"

I finally found my voice. "You're offering me a job?"

"I'm not sure yet. We should talk. My name's Bobby." He reached out his hand for me to shake.

The next day I'd met Bobby at his office in Malibu and he talked to me about Saddles & Racks and what they had to offer. He was the LA head person and Mark was the Vegas person.

"Why was he at a shit bar?" Nancy asked.

I laughed. "I asked him the same thing. He said it was where he found all his recruits. Like diamonds in the rough or some shit."

"But not Candy."

We both laughed. "No, not Candy. Thank God for Bobby or I might have the herp." I was half-joking. I might have had enough money for her to blow me that night.

"Things happen for a reason."

"Yeah, they do."

We ordered another round of drinks, talked some more, and then I convinced Nancy to leave with me so her friends would think we were hooking up and I walked her to her car.

When I got home to my empty house, my phone buzzed with a text from Mark.

Mark: *You okay with a new roommate?*

Well, shit, that was fast.

Me: *Yeah sure, whatever.*

Mark: *Cool. Andy will be there next week sometime.*

Chapter Five

Joselyn

It had been twelve years since I'd been back to Miami. Since the night I fled, I hadn't returned. When the taxi dropped me off at the bus station, I bought a one-way ticket to Washington D.C.

I'd barely made the last bus for the night, and when I asked how long it would take for me to get there, I wasn't expecting to be told twenty-seven hours. I had no clothes other than what I was wearing. No toothbrush, no brush to comb my hair, no food—nothing. Luckily, I had the wad of cash I'd stolen from Marco and I had over thirteen hundred dollars left after my bus ticket. Who the hell carried that much cash on them? Maybe it was to pay for our date. I had a feeling it wasn't, though. I didn't know Tony, but the way he was dressed, the way he spoke to me, the limo he picked me up in, and his bodyguard Jose all indicated that one's virginity was worth more than a few hundred dollars, especially if he were splitting it with my mother. The hotel room probably cost more for one night than the cash in Marco's wallet.

The bus pulled to a stop, jolting and squeaking, causing me to wake.

"We're here."

I looked to my left toward Alison. She had become my friend in the short amount of time we'd traveled from Miami to D.C. She hadn't asked why I was crying when she'd first met me. Instead, she'd started talking to me at our first rest stop about poutine fries she'd had in Canada, and she made me laugh. Gravy and cheese curds on French fries? What had the world come to? She swore up and down that it was the best thing ever and that I needed to try it. I was a chili and cheese girl myself. Granted that was only in the summer when Seth treated me.

"What time is it?" I yawned.

"Almost two in the morning."

Where the hell was I supposed to go at two in the morning? I had no way of contacting Seth. I didn't know what precinct he was at. Didn't know his phone number, where he lived, or if he was even on duty.

I nodded and stood, ready to get off the bus and wander around a city I didn't know.

"Do you need my mom to take you somewhere?" Alison asked.

"My friend should be here to pick me up," I lied. How would I explain to her mother why I was dressed like a hooker? How would I tell her I needed to go to every police station until I found Seth? I felt as if I had a big sign above my head and it was flashing that I was just sold to the highest bidder.

"Want us to wait until they show up?"

We began walking down the aisle toward the front of the bus in a single file. "No, no, it's late. I'm sure he's here."

"Give me your cell number and I'll program mine. We should hang out sometime."

I almost began to cry again. I wanted so badly to be normal. I was seventeen and I should have a cell phone. This day and age practically everyone had a cell phone. "I—"

Her gaze met mine. "Silly me. You probably left it with your stuff in Miami. Let me find some paper and a pen and I'll write mine down for you." I knew I would never call her. The fewer people who knew who I was (and who knew I was in D.C.) the better.

I didn't know if she did it on purpose, but I was grateful she was quick not to question why I didn't have a phone or any belongings. I was sure she saw it written on my imaginary neon sign that I was a hot mess. I felt as if I were one. I was broken and still sore as fuck between my legs. My feet hurt like a bitch in those god awful heels too. I couldn't wait until I got to take a nice long bath followed by a long cry in a bed before I slept for a week.

After Alison and her mother left, I grabbed a waiting taxi and asked to be taken to the closest police station. The driver eyed me through the rearview mirror. It didn't faze me. The last forty-eight hours had been the worst of my life and having another taxi driver wonder what was going on with me wasn't bothering me one bit. I was finally in the same city as my best friend. Granted it was a huge city and I had no idea where he was.

I stared out the window watching the orange streetlights as the driver took me to the precinct. Theoretically, I didn't know if it was the closest one to the bus station, but it didn't matter. What were the odds that I'd walk in and it'd be Seth's station? What were the odds that he'd be on duty at this hour or even at the station?

The taxi pulled up to the front of the station and I asked him to wait a few minutes while I ran inside. I took a deep breath and then walked up the concrete stairs. My heart was racing. Even though I'd had over a day to plan out what I was going to tell Seth, I hadn't really thought about what I was going to say to him. "I ran away, you're taking me in. The end."

Before I reached my hand out for the door, I turned slightly to make sure the taxi was still there. He was. Of course he was. He wanted his cab fare. But I wanted this police station to be the station where my best friend was so I could cry in his arms and feel safe. Seth always made me feel safe and I really needed him. I wasn't the adult I thought I was. I didn't care that I had less than a year until I was legally an adult. I needed … I needed to know everything was going to be okay.

Taking another deep breath, I reached up and tugged on the door, but it didn't budge. "What the fuck?" I murmured. I tugged on the other door, but it too didn't open. My heart instantly dropped. I knew it was a long shot to show up, but I hadn't expected the police station to be closed. I peered through the glass window trying to find anyone who could help me. I didn't see anyone.

My eyes started to sting, my chest began to tighten and my head started to feel fuzzy. This wasn't happening. How could I travel over a day and then show up at a police station only to find it closed? Weren't they supposed to be there to help you?

The sound of honking brought me out of my daze and I jumped. "Miss!" I turned and saw that the cabbie had yelled through the rolled down window. "You need to pay me."

I hurried down the steps, needing to decide what to do next. "Sorry," I breathed as I slid into the car.

"Where to now?"

I closed my eyes briefly, fighting back the tears. It wasn't the time for them.

"Well?" he asked.

"Just… Just give me a minute."

"Meter's running," he reminded me.

I opened my eyes to find he was looking at me through the rearview mirror. "Is there like a Walmart or something?"

"You want me to take you shopping?" he asked.

"Look…" I looked at his name that was on his licenses stuck to the glass divider, but I couldn't pronounce it. "I had a long bus ride from Miami. I left all my stuff there. Please take me to a Walmart that's open to buy some clothes and toiletries, then take me to a motel, okay? I'll tip you good, I promise." Teenage hormones, lack of sleep, the last few days—everything all rolled into one was creeping up on me and I really didn't know how much more I could take before I broke down and stayed in the back of the taxi forever. He nodded and pulled onto the street without another word. When we arrived at the store, he turned slightly and told me he was stopping the meter while I ran inside. I didn't question him. Maybe he felt bad because I was crying. I thanked him and hurried in. I grabbed a few shirts, a pair of jeans, flip-flops, panties, a bra (damn, I'd been dying for a bra), pajamas and the toiletries I'd need to get me through the next few days in case I couldn't find Seth.

Afterward, the cab driver drove me to the nearest motel. At first they were hesitant to rent me a room without a driver's license or any I.D. Right away the tears started to flow, but I explained the situation; it was almost four in the morning and I only wanted it for a few hours. When I said those words, I cringed. I was still dressed in my short, strapless dress, heels and I had no doubt my makeup was long gone. I knew that damn neon sign was still flashing above my head.

Finally, they agreed to rent me a room. Once I locked myself in, I took a long shower where I cried on the base of the tub with the water spraying down on me. I didn't cry for long, though. I was too tired.

The moment my head hit the pillow, I fell asleep.

I woke to the sound of knocking and a lady announcing she was housekeeping. Glancing at the clock, I realized that it was after noon and I was supposed to have checked out of the room by now.

"Coming!" I replied. I hurried to the door. "Sorry," I apologized, unlocking it after I'd made sure it was housekeeping through the peephole. "I overslept. Can you give me ten minutes? I need to get dressed."

She nodded and pushed her cart to the next room. I hurried to change. Everything was happening too fast and I still didn't know what I was going to say to Seth when I saw him, but I knew I needed to find him. I needed to find him before nightfall because I didn't want to be homeless. Being homeless wasn't part of the plan. Actually none of this was. Why did my mother do this? Why did I do this?

As I gathered all my stuff, it hit me that at least back in Miami I'd have a roof over my head. Granted, I'd have to spread my legs after doing homework. A tear fell and I wiped it before I grabbed the two plastic bags that held the only belongings to my name and left the room in search of my best friend.

The police station the cab driver had taken me to only a few hours before was a few blocks away. I walked there after grabbing a bagel and coffee. It was lunch time, but to me it was breakfast time and I was starving. Everything was so fucked up and I had no idea when or if things would turn around.

When I made it to the precinct, the door opened on the first try. I wasn't nervous until I'd taken my first step inside. Part of me had thought the station would still be closed. I expected all eyes to be on me, my neon sign flashing, but no one looked at me as I walked up to the desk that was closed off by what I assumed was a bullet proof glass. The clerk looked up after I stood there for what seemed like a full minute.

"Can I help you?"

"I'm looking for Officer McKenna," I stated nervously, not meeting her gaze.

"We don't have an officer by that name."

My heart fell through the pit of my stomach and onto the white tiled floor. Of course, the first precinct wouldn't be where he worked. I sighed.

"Do you have a crime to report?"

I did. A crime that they couldn't help with. A crime that I couldn't tell anyone about—ever. I shook my head. "No."

"Then we can't help you."

I sighed again and swallowed back the disappointment. "Can you at least give me the address or addresses of the other stations?" She groaned, but she grabbed a piece of paper and wrote a few addresses down for me. "Would you mind calling me a cab?" I asked and gave a tight smile. I had a feeling I was walking a fine line by asking for so much help that wasn't crime related.

"You can go outside and flag one down," she responded sarcastically.

I had no idea and felt stupid for asking. I nodded and turned to leave. When I went outside, cars whizzed by, but I saw a yellow cab, so I raised my arm and waved for it to stop. It pulled over and I slid in.

On the way to the next station, I thought about what I would say to Seth in case I did get lucky and it was his precinct. He knew how much I hated my mother. He saw firsthand how mean she was to me on numerous occasions. I could blame one of those times and the fact that I was a teenager, but how could I explain how I got the bus money to make the trip?

Before I could think about it further, the cab pulled to a stop at the next station. I paid and exited the taxi. I didn't ask for it to wait. If this wasn't the correct one, I'd flag down another cab. I entered the station and walked up to the counter like I had at the last station. "I'm looking for Officer McKenna."

The desk officer pointed behind me and my eyes became huge as I held my breath and turned. He was walking through the doors with another officer.

"McKenna!"

I jumped at the sudden yell from behind me. Seth's gaze met mine and his eyes widened. "Joss?" he asked. "Shit!" He rushed to me and grabbed my hand without another word, leading me outside to a parking lot and to a police cruiser. "Inside!" he barked when he unlocked the doors with the key fob.

This wasn't what I was expecting. I wanted him to hug me; wrap me in his arms and tell me it was going to be okay. Tell me that I didn't have to go back and live with Cruella any longer.

"Seth—"

"Just wait, Joselyn."

Fuck. He'd used my full first name. This wasn't going to be good. I was fighting back the tears yet again. I hadn't cried so much in my life and I feared I'd never stop. My world felt as if it were ending and everything and everyone was against me—even my best friend.

I glanced at him a few times as he navigated the streets in silence. I wanted to ask him why he wasn't questioning me about being there; it wasn't like I'd showed up for afternoon tea. We finally pulled into an apartment complex and after he'd parked, he grabbed my two plastic bags.

"Is this all you have?"

I nodded. Before I could slide out of the car completely, he came around and reached for my hand, finally pulling me into the hug I longed for. My throat tightened as I continued to fight the tears that were pricking my eyes, but there was no use. They spilled over and I started to cry against his shoulder. I felt safe for the first time in seventy-two hours. I was crushed hard against him, pressed into things that were hurting me, but I didn't want to move.

This was Seth.

My Seth.

"Grandma called and said you never came home on your birthday," he murmured into my hair. "I was trying to get some of the guys to cover my shifts so I could go down to help look for you."

"I ran away," I whispered.

"Come inside." He kissed the top of my head before he reached for my hand and led me toward his apartment.

"Why are you mad at me?" I asked.

"I was surprised to see you." He reached up and wiped a tear from my cheek.

"But you didn't talk to me the whole way here."

"I was thinking, Josie. I have so many questions, but it's better if we talk in my apartment." He nudged his head toward his car.

I didn't know what he meant. Cameras? Audio? I let him lead me to his apartment. Once we entered, he set my bags down and I looked around the living room while he went to the kitchen. I finally smiled because this was definitely his apartment. A big screen TV hung on the wall across from a giant sectional couch. On the coffee table, empty beer bottles sat scattered, but what made me smile was that the picture that I kept in my purse of the three of us was framed and sitting on the end table next to the couch.

"Here." He handed me a glass of water. "Sit and tell me what happened."

I took the glass and looked at him for a beat. "Do … Do you have to be dressed like that?" He still looked like the Seth I remembered, only a little older.

He had the same short dark brown hair that was almost black and the same sea green eyes. The only thing that had changed was the stubble from a lightly trimmed goatee that framed his perfect smile and teeth. And his body... well, he was a cop who worked the streets. I was sure his tight uniform covered a nice body.

"Josie." He smiled.

"I ran away and you're dressed like a cop." I waved a hand in his direction.

"I am a cop." He reminded me.

"Am I in trouble?" The question had spilled from my lips before I knew it. I wasn't sure what my mother had told his grandma. I was a minor who had run away after all.

He looked straight into my eyes. I wanted to tear my gaze from his. I didn't like that he was dressed in his uniform. I couldn't take it. I had a feeling I was in trouble. If he wanted to take me back, I was going to beg him to let me stay. If he forced me to go back, I didn't know what I would do.

"No." He shook his head. "I'll go change, but you need to tell me what really happened, okay?"

I swallowed. "O-Okay."

When he returned, he was dressed in jeans and a black T-shirt. He looked more like my best friend than a cop interrogating me. He sat back down on the section of the couch diagonal from me. "Okay. What happened?" He reached for my hand and ran his thumb over mine.

"Cruella and I got into a fight and I left." I shrugged.

He chuckled. "Joss, you didn't run away because of a fight. You two fight all the time. What really happened? And how the hell did you get here?"

I looked up and met his sea green eyes. "What did your grandma tell you?"

He tilted his head a little. "She said your mom told her you didn't return after dinner." I gave a sarcastic chuckle. "What's so funny?"

"Come on, Seth!" I stood out of anger, breaking our contact. "Who the hell was I supposed to have dinner with? You know Cat's in Hawaii, she probably doesn't even know I'm missing. I didn't have dinner with anyone. Cruella told your grandma that, but I didn't have any birthday dinner plans."

"Grandma said she saw you get into a limo."

And there was the swallow. It was, in fact, me swallowing my lie. "I went around the block while Cruella got ready for her date. She had a date on my birthday. You know she doesn't care about me. When she got home, I left. I'd had enough. I can't take her shit anymore, Seth. It was my birthday and she left in a limo to have a date. She didn't even wish me a happy birthday." More tears streamed down my face. Part of what I was saying was true and it still hurt.

He stood and wrapped me in his arms. "You can't leave because you got in a fight. You're seventeen. You need to go back and finish school."

"I'll stay here and get my GED."

"You need to go back. If anyone finds out that you're here—"

I pulled my head back. "What do you mean?"

"I'm a cop and there are laws. You're seventeen. You have to be in school. And you ran away from home, Josie."

"Like I said, I'll get my GED."

He took a deep breath. "Fuck, Joss. This isn't good. Cruella's gonna be pissed."

"She's not going to care." Little did he know, she would. She was going to be livid. "You don't even need to tell her I'm here. She's probably happy I'm gone. One less mouth to feed."

"I'm going to call Grandma and tell her—"

"No!" I shrieked and reached for his arm as he stepped away from me. I didn't want him to call her. Before I could utter another word, his cell rang.

"It's her."

My heart stopped. I was screwed. I was one hundred and twenty-thousand percent screwed. This was the end of the road. He would tell her I was here, she'd tell Mother, and then I'd be on my way back to Miami to start my new career.

"Hey, Grandma, I have good news ...What?" he exclaimed and my head snapped in his direction. My gaze met his. "Are you sure?" He ran a hand down his face. "Everything? ... Boxes? ... Bryce too?" I sat down on the couch. "Okay. Let me know if you find out anything else. Oh, right." He smiled and I smiled back. This was a good sign. At least I thought it was. "Joss is here ... Yeah. I'm not sure, but she is. She got into a fight with Maggie and ran away ... I'll take care of her until we find out. Okay, I'll tell her. Love you, too. Bye."

"What'd she say?" I asked as soon as he pressed a button on his cell.

"Your mom and brother are gone."

"What do you mean gone?"

"They left with some guys." I blinked at him, not saying anything. "Joss?"

"Are you sure?"

"Grandma went over to check and the door was unlocked. Everything was boxed up and gone."

I didn't know what to say. What did it mean? Why would Tony take them? And then it hit me like a ton of bricks:

"...you and your mother are going to pay."

"What are you thinking about?"

I stopped swirling my straw in my iced tea and watched as Seth slid into the seat across from me. There was no way I was going to tell him that I was thinking about twelve years ago. He still didn't know why I'd run away. After we'd found out that my mother and brother left, we'd waited a few days, but they never returned. In fact, Seth's grandma told us the trailer was cleaned out and rented to a new family. She never saw them again. *I* never saw them again. I'd tried to search for them in our database but always came up short.

"Just a case." I shrugged.

"You want to talk about it?" He smirked.

"Then I'd have to kill you."

"Well, we wouldn't want that."

Seth still worked for the DCPD as a detective, so he knew I couldn't talk about it. I eventually became a cop as well, but my heart was focused on special crimes and becoming a part of the Federal Bureau of Investigation. I wanted… No, I *needed* to make a difference when it came to crimes against children. At first it was hard to stomach some of the cases I was assigned, but it fueled my fire.

"How was your date last night?" I asked, changing the subject.

"I'd tell you, but then I'd have to kill you."

"Please. You'd miss me too much." I smirked.

"This is true."

"So?" I prompted.

"The better question is, when are you going to go on a date?"

All right so this subject needed to change. "Oh shit, look at the time. I have a meeting."

He laughed and I fought back my own. "You're so full of shit."

The truth was I hadn't dated much in the last twelve years. The bigger truth was that I hadn't slept with any of my boyfriends. Those boyfriends never lasted; none of them ever wanted to stick around. I was twenty-nine now and none of them wanted to wait until it got serious. When it got hot and heavy and I pulled away, they would say they understood and then wouldn't see me anymore. Seth and I remained best friends over the years. I needed him as a friend and couldn't lose him, so I didn't want to jeopardize our friendship by starting a relationship. Plus, he never once acted as though he wanted more and I never mentioned it either. I wasn't even attracted to him anymore. He was my family.

"Bye, jerk face!" I punched him in the arm as I walked by.

"Big baby!" he whined as he rubbed his arm and I laughed.

We'd had plans for lunch, but I was always running from my seventeenth birthday, even when it came to my best friend.

Later that afternoon I really did have a meeting. I sat at the mahogany table with my black, leather portfolio in front of me. I stared at my phone, checking my emails as everyone started to file in.

"We have a new case," my boss, Eric, informed us. I opened my notepad. "In the United States alone, there are over thirty-five hundred sex trafficking cases reported each year. Worldwide on average about twenty-two hundred girls are kidnapped every single day and forced into the sex trade. They are beaten, raped and almost always killed. On average, a single girl will be raped six thousand times and only have a life expectancy of seven years until she is killed by her ring leader. The odds of her being rescued is one out of a hundred. Word on the street is that women are being taken for sex trafficking in Las Vegas. We don't have all the details, but we need to find out who's behind this and where the women are being sold to. My cousin runs an escort business in Vegas, so that's where we'll start."

"Is this a legit escort business?" Ella asked.

Eric nodded. "I've run some checks on his business and he knows who I work for. The Green family reunion would be awkward if it weren't." We chuckled.

"What's the business called?" Brent asked.

"Saddles & Racks." We all stifled our laughs. "I know what you're all thinking, but they're paid for companionship only."

I sat quietly as I listened to everyone chatter. I'd never been to Vegas and had no idea what was involved in an escort business, but I knew if it was anything like Tony's business, sex was *definitely* involved.

"I need either Ella or Joselyn to go undercover and see if you can find out what's going on."

My hand immediately shot up.

"Perfect. Joss, you leave next week. We'll get you a new identity and a place to live. You'll be undercover until you have something."

I nodded. I'd never been undercover, but this was my chance to finally make a difference or at least try to make a difference when it came to prostitution. Being in the thick of things was going to light my fire more. Since that night I was sold, I'd felt it was my duty to save them all. And if I was able to get one girl off the streets, then that was one girl who would have a better life.

During the week, I tied up loose ends and told Seth what I could about my new assignment. It wasn't much. He knew I was going undercover, but he didn't know where. I gave him Ella's cell number in case anything happened while I was away; that was the only way to get information to me. The bureau also had me take a few lessons in self-defense while wearing high heels. At first I'd thought it was crazy until I realized it was hard to fight off an attacker in those things.

I tried not to think about what I was getting involved with. I knew if I thought about it, I would become nervous and start to freak out. I was going to be involved with girls who were being sold—*just like I had been sold.* I was lucky to get out, but now I was going back in. Hopefully to save as many girls as I could.

When the day finally came and I boarded my flight for Vegas. I didn't board it as Joselyn Marquez.

I boarded it as Andi Middlebrooke.

Chapter Six

Paul

Throughout the week, I waited for that Andy guy to show. Delivery men showed up with his shit, but he had yet to arrive. What kind of guy couldn't move his own stuff? I was already dreading meeting my new roommate. If he was some fancy motherfucker, we weren't going to get along. Men needed to be manly. We were made to lift heavy stuff. God forbid we broke a nail.

I wasn't sure if I needed to be home when this guy showed up or what, but I still had work to do. This afternoon I had a unique date. When I'd read the details in my back office on my phone, I'd laughed. Tanja had hired me for three hours to be a naked chef while she had a book club at her house. I wasn't required to cook (thank God). She would have platters of food for me to serve.

Normally any date I would dress to impress, but since this one I'd be naked, I threw on a pair of grey cargo shorts and a maroon T-shirt before driving to the address provided. When I arrived, I was greeted with a bright smile.

"Howzit?" Tanja greeted.

I chuckled. "Hi." I stepped forward and gave her a hug.

"Please come in."

"Where's your accent from?"

She smiled as she closed the door behind us. "I'm from South Africa."

"No shit?" She nodded and I followed her toward what I guessed to be the kitchen. "What has you in Vegas?"

"My husband had a job opportunity and we took it. Better education for our children, too."

I nodded. "So uh," I rubbed the back of my neck, "does he know you hired me?"

She laughed and it was the first time I saw her dimples on each cheek—I had a thing for a woman's smile. "It was his idea."

I drew my head back, not expecting that answer. "Really?"

"He's hoping this spices things up in the bedroom."

"I see. So he wants you to get horny and fuck his brains out?"

"Pretty much."

"I'm sure that can be arranged."

"Perfect." She bit her lip and a blush crept up her neck before she turned and started to put the food together.

I helped Tanja arrange the finger foods on platters, and just as we finished the doorbell rang. She smiled again and held up a black half apron. "You can change in the bathroom around the corner. Remember, only the apron. Nothing else."

"I gotcha, sugar."

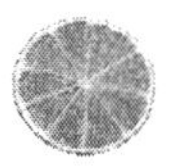

Those ladies were feisty. I had no idea that women in book clubs were so horny. All they talked about was how my body compared to those of book boyfriends. What the hell was a book boyfriend?

When I would bend over to serve one of the ladies, another would cop a feel. I was all for it, but it was turning me on. The closer their hands got to my dick, the harder I was getting. I wasn't hiding it and they loved it.

When I arrived home, I pulled my *Jeep* into the garage and then headed to my room to take a shower. I was tired and really needed to rub one out before my dick fell off. After lifting my T-shirt from my chest, the doorbell rang. I wanted to ignore it, but it rang again. I groaned as I left my room and went down the hall. This was probably Andy. He was already pissing me off and I hadn't even met the guy. It was late in the evening and I knew it was Vegas—one of the cities that never slept, but seriously, he was an escort too. What if I was still on my date?

Before I reached the door, it rang again. "Jesus," I barked. "I'm coming!" I swung the door open. "I heard you…" I stopped yelling. It wasn't Andy, it was a woman—a fucking hot woman, and I was already horny as fuck.

"Are you going to let me in or are you going to leave me standing on the porch?"

I looked around her to see if she was with Andy. She was alone with luggage. *Who the hell was this chick?*

"Do you speak?"

"Yes, I speak," I snapped. "Who are you and why the fuck do you want in my house?"

"I'm Andi, you're new roommate."

I laughed. "Is this a joke? Andy's a dude's name and you're a woman."

She groaned. "Well, I see this is going to work out well." She brushed passed me. "It's Andi with an I. How about you just show me to my room, Einstein? It's been a long day."

I closed the door behind me and gestured for her to follow. She reached for her luggage to wheel to her room, but I waved her hand away to carry it down the hall.

"You don't need to do that."

"Seems we got off on the wrong foot. I'm sorry, I didn't know my new roommate was going to be a woman."

"Is it going to be a problem?"

The only problem I could think of at the moment was her naked across the hall from me every day. I wasn't sure if it was because I was aching down below or because she was painfully stunning. She had long, dark brown hair, her face was lightly speckled with freckles, and her eyes were cognac.

"No, we're both adults." I walked her down the hall. "So ah, here you go." I turned on the light to her room that was my old room—my old room where I could picture her naked …

Fuck me.

"Thanks. Sorry for showing up this late. I had a few layovers."

"No worries. I wasn't doing anything," I lied. I stood there and watched as she took in the space as if she'd never seen the items in the room before. I placed the luggage on her bed. "Well, I'll let you settle in. If you need anything, I'll be across the hall." *Thinking about you.*

"Thanks again."

Once in my room and behind closed doors, I hurried and stripped myself of all my clothes. Fuck, this wasn't good. How could Mark not tell me that Andy was *Andi*? It didn't matter. Like I'd said, we were both adults. Maybe if I weren't going out of my mind and needing release, things would be different. The last two dates I hadn't slept with the women. It was all relative, but I still had hopes and *needs.*

The spray of the warm shower cascaded down my toned, chiseled abs as my head hung and I thought about what Andi was doing only a few feet away. I knew I shouldn't. I didn't know anything about her, but she was fucking gorgeous and I was hard as rock.

I thought about her tight waist in her hip-hugger jeans and the way I would unbutton them, her eyes peering down on me as I slid them over her perfect ass and down her legs. My dick ached as I imagined myself picking her up and placing her on the queen size bed in her room, her legs wrapping around me and her hand reaching to stroke me.

My hand mimicked how I imagined hers would glide over my glistening shaft, her soft hand squeezing just enough as I brought my mouth to hers and kissed her feverishly. I heard myself groan, my hand stroking faster, flashes of her face dancing behind my closed lids as the water helped my hand move over my dick.

The water rushed down my body into my hand. The heat of the stream was exactly how I envisioned her mouth would be as she slid down my body to use it on my shaft. I wanted her perfect, sassy mouth wrapped around my aching dick as if it was my next breath. She was a feisty little thing, and dammit if it didn't turn me on more.

Stroking faster and faster, I couldn't last much longer—I didn't want to. I wanted to come hard inside her brazen mouth. I reached up with my free hand, placed it on the tiled wall in front of me and braced myself as my balls tightened, my legs weakened and I groaned again, shooting cum into the shower spray.

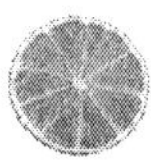

The next morning I woke early, thinking I'd beat Andi so I could make breakfast—a peace offering. When I walked into the kitchen, she was sitting at the kitchen table, drinking coffee, and her long hair was in a messy thingy on top of her head.

This was going to be hard on my dick.

Fuck!

"You're up early." I opened the cabinet and grabbed a coffee mug.

"On D.C. time I guess."

I poured the black heaven into my coffee mug. "I didn't know S&R had a location in D.C."

She took a sip of her coffee before responding. "They don't. I was with another company."

"Oh, I see. So you decided to try your *luck* out here in Vegas?" I slid into the chair in front of her at the table and stared into her eyes—they were definitely on the lighter honey brown side. She smiled and I determined that it was my mission to make her smile every second of every day. It was my favorite part of a woman's body, and Andi's smile was perfect.

"Something like that. How long have you been with S&R?"

"Too long." I chuckled. "How about I buy you breakfast and we can talk all about it?"

"You want to buy me breakfast?"

"Sure why not?"

"Don't you work?"

I laughed. "As in a date?"

She blushed. "Oh, right."

I wasn't sure why she blushed or why she seemed confused. Maybe her old company had weird hours. We had day dates, of course, but it was usually after coffee. "How long have you been an escort?"

She took another sip of her coffee. "Not that long."

"Might need to show you some of my moves." She choked on her coffee. "Are you okay? I was only joking."

When she could speak again, she said, "Yeah, I'm fine. You sleep with your clients?"

"Aw, gorgeous, you think I'm gonna tell you all my secrets when we've just met?" I smirked.

"Will you if I let you buy me breakfast?"

"Oh, you're good."

She stood and went to the dishwasher. "I'm going to go change so I can learn your dirty secrets."

I watched her ass as she walked down the hall to her bedroom. Having Andi as a roommate was going to be much better than having a dog.

Chapter Seven

Andi

If I could march into the office back in D.C., I would rip Eric a new one. I didn't care if he was my boss. How dare he place me in a house with a man and not a woman? I didn't care if I was twenty-nine. Who does that? There had to have been a better solution than sending me to a strange city to live with Paul.

The entire week leading up to me moving to Vegas, I'd researched Saddles & Racks. I'd memorized every escort they had. So when Paul opened the door, I knew exactly who he was. I didn't know he lived in the house until he said he didn't know his new roommate was going to be a woman. His address was in the file, of course, but he wasn't on my radar when I researched S&R so I didn't recognize my new address. Plus I had flown across the country and I was dead tired when I'd arrive. Let alone the fact he had been shirtless when he'd opened the door and I'd lost all train of thought. I didn't know my new roommate was going to look like sin in the form of a man who could ride me…

Gah, what the hell was I thinking?

I'd just met the man and I hadn't had sex since that dreadful night, but the thought of Paul's chest and abs when he opened the door sent a tingle to my toes that started in my belly and I was instantly on defense. I knew I was a bitch to him, but I'd had to be. That's what I'd become.

I changed my tactic because I had to get info out of him. I woke up early—well, early for west coast time—grabbed a coffee and reviewed my notes. When Paul came out (shirtless *again*), I tried to get him to tell me about some of his clients. He wouldn't, of course.

So I settled for breakfast.

"How long do I have to wait for your dirty secrets?"

Paul stopped mid-bite of his scrambled eggs. "You know we met less than twenty-four hours ago, right?"

I shrugged. "I figured since we're going to be roommates that we should get them over with." That wasn't true. Earlier when we were talking about secrets, it had slipped out. Now I was trying to keep the conversation going over breakfast.

"Are you going to tell me yours?" He smirked.

No. "Maybe." I took a sip of my orange juice.

He eyed me for a few beats and I got the sense that he was looking deep into my soul. I wasn't used to it. I was used to being the one reading people; I'd learned it from Seth. Over the years, he'd taught me how to get answers, to learn the truth. We were good at our jobs.

The longer Paul stared at me, the more nervous I became. I was mid-sip of my OJ when he asked, "Should we just fuck and get it over with?"

The juice went down the wrong pipe and I began to choke. "Oh my God," I gasped, coughing between words.

"Are you okay?"

"What's wrong with you?" I asked, still coughing, my eyes watering.

"You want to know my dirty secrets. That's the best way to find out."

I stared at him, the coughing coming in spurts. "That's not what I meant." He started laughing and then ate an entire turkey sausage link. "Why are you laughing?"

"This is going to be fun."

"What is?"

"Well, my last roommates were a couple. Gabe was my best friend and knew all my tricks, so I wasn't able to fuck with him. Then Auttie came into the picture and he'd cut my balls off if I tried to mess with her, so I wasn't able to do anything, but you—man …" He shook his head and smiled. "We're just getting started!"

I stared at him.

"What?" he asked.

"Should I be scared?"

He smirked. "No, gorgeous, you should be flattered."

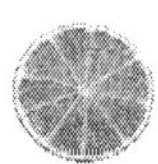

I wasn't sure why I was being brave with Paul. This wasn't like me. Even if it was all talk, it wasn't like me to even talk about sex. Sex wasn't something that came into conversation until the third date and then I skated around it as if it were lobster and I had a food allergy.

But for some reason, Paul made it seem natural.

He was sin…

Dripping with hot, hot sin …

I'd heard that a woman's sex drive really kicked into gear in her thirties. I was approaching thirty and I felt that sucker kicking. Or in this case, dripping.

Drip.

Drip.

Drip.

Fuck.

Fuck.

Fuck.

The problem? I wasn't sure I could physically be with him or anyone even if I wanted to be.

I didn't know how to be an escort. Hell, I didn't even know how to go on dates in general. Luckily, I reached out to two of the female escorts who worked for S&R. I needed to get some kind of info or my first date was bound to be a disaster; my first date which was tonight.

Yeah, I was screwed.

I only had two girlfriends. One was Ella from work and we didn't hang out much, just chatted a little while at work. The other girl was Cat. She was still living in Miami and I only saw her once a year. When she got back from Hawaii, she'd called Seth and we told her about my fight with Cruella. I knew they both thought there was more to the story, but I never told them the truth. I couldn't. No one could ever know. My world would be over and everything around me would come crashing down as my flaws surfaced. I would never be the same.

Shaking off the thought, I took a taxi to where I was meeting Leah and Nina for lunch. I needed to get a car. That was next on the list of things to do. I'd left mine in D.C. because Eric told me I could pick up a car when I arrived so I didn't have to drive across the country in mine.

The taxi dropped me off in front of the Thai restaurant down on Fremont Street. I immediately recognized the two women. They both had russet brown hair and dark tans. I groaned as I stared down at my frosty, pale arms and legs. I was going to stand out as though I had a vitamin D deficiency next to these two. Leah was a petite Hawaiian woman originally from the Bay Area in California. Nina was originally from Houston, Texas. She wasn't much taller than Leah, but she was more muscular. Her FBI file stated she competed in fitness competitions.

Before I reached them, they turned and saw me and waved. I didn't know how they knew it was me, but then I remembered that my picture was plastered on the S&R website and they probably looked me up just as I had them, though my search for them was a little more intense as I'd looked into their criminal records.

"I hope you like strip clubs," Leah said, greeting me with a hug. My eyes widened as I embraced her. I'd never been to a strip club before. Was this my life now that I was in Sin City? Were nights spent on dates in strip clubs? Was I to take dates to strip clubs?

"Are we talking men or women?" I asked, trying to sound normal. *Crap.*

"Oh, you're into ladies, too?" Nina asked, giving me a quick hug.

I swallowed hard and shook off my shock. Working as a cop and then FBI, I'd been in strip clubs and busted perps, but I'd never been to one where I had to dress the part to hang out and do God knows what. I'd obviously needed more than a week to prepare myself for this undercover mission. *Maybe I was in way over my head.* Before I could answer, the hostess brought us back to the patio in the back. We were seated under water misters and the question was forgotten.

"So have you been to a female strip club?" Lea asked.

Well, I'd hoped that the question was forgotten. "Is this what Vegas is all about?" I asked, scanning the menu and trying not to make eye contact.

They laughed. I didn't get the joke.

"We need to get you clients, right?" Nina asked. I lifted my gaze and nodded. "So this is how we do it in Vegas when we're just starting out. We go to a female strip club, and while the chicks dance, we hit on the horny bastards watching, slip them our cards, and then wait for them to call."

"I don't have any cards," I admitted.

"Mark should have them for you today," Leah informed, then took a sip of her water.

I hadn't thought about needing to get clients. The more I thought about it, though, the more I realized that having clients and getting in with other girls would allow me to investigate how things were run around the city. I couldn't wait for things to come to me.

I had to go to them.

Chapter Eight

Paul

My smile hadn't faltered since breakfast. I enjoyed messing around with Andi, and I wasn't even fucking her…

Yet.

The more I made her smile, the more I couldn't concentrate on anything but her. I wanted to lean across the table at breakfast and taste the orange juice on her lips, but my gut told me that she was guarding *something.*

We were escorts, but not all escorts slept around. I didn't feel right asking her if she slept with her clients. The thought of her being with someone else made my stomach churn and I didn't know why. *What was wrong with me? I just met this chick.* So I sat back and joked around with her instead of asking her for real. Granted, I did ask her to fuck me and if she would have said yes, I would have said, "Check, please!" and dragged her ass into the *Jeep* and fucked her right there in the back with her legs spread wide and me balls deep.

But she hadn't and when we went home, she did her thing and I left to meet Gabe and Autumn at the range.

I needed to talk to Gabe.

When I got to the range, I knew my smile was still plastered across my face. I usually had one. I hid my sorrows well. It was confirmed when Auttie saw me.

"Someone's happy," she observed.

"I'm always happy."

She shook her auburn brown hair ponytail and scrunched her eyebrows. "No, you're like *overly* happy."

Gabe clapped me on the back. "He got laid."

Autumn chuckled. "What's new?" She started to get her gun ready while we watched.

"I think I found my match."

Gabe's head tilted a little. The popping of gunfire could be heard in the distance of the outdoor range. "Your match?"

"Andi."

His eyebrows furrowed. "Who's Andi?"

"I think I'm in love." I wasn't in love, but like me at first, I knew he'd think Andi was a dude. "Andi, man. I could look at that ass all day!"

His green eyes blinked at me. "What? You're in love with a man?"

I saw Autumn set her gun down on the wood shooting bench and walk the few feet to us. "Did you just say that you're in love with a man?"

I laughed a full-on belly laugh. "Andi's a chick and my new roommate. Mark sent a girl to live with me."

"When do I get to meet her?" Autumn asked.

"She just moved in last night, Auttie."

She shrugged. "And?"

"And—"

"So you haven't fucked her already?" Gabe asked.

I shook my head. "No, but man, she's feisty and I like it."

Gabe stared at me for a few seconds. "Does this mean you're ready to move on from Vanessa?"

I gave a sarcastic laugh. "I'm over that bitch."

"Whatever, PJ. You're my best friend. You haven't dated anyone the entire time I've known you. You think you've never told me about Vanessa?"

I stared back at him. I didn't remember discussing Vanessa with him, especially in detail. We'd always dealt with *his* problems. If he hadn't gotten help, he would have drunk himself to death. Luckily, Autumn had bumped into him at the right time and showed him that there was more to living than a bottle of whiskey every night.

"You don't even know what that bitch did to me."

"You've told me a few times while you've been drunk."

"Whatever," I huffed.

"We all have our demons, PJ. You were there for mine. I'm here to help you with yours if you're ready for that. Maybe Andi's here," he pulled Autumn to his side and kissed the top of her head, "to show you that your first love is not always meant to be your last."

I shook my head. "Again, I just met her last night. Let's not get ahead of ourselves."

He nodded and cracked a smile. "I wasn't the one declaring my love five minutes ago."

I narrowed my eyes at him and rolled my eyes. "Touché, Cap. Touché."

"Are you two girls ready to shoot or what?" Autumn asked.

As I drove home, I thought about what Gabe had said. I hadn't really thought about Vanessa in years. Sure I'd thought about her, but I hadn't *thought* about her.

I couldn't.

Each time I did, I thought about what it meant to kill a part of me, to take that decision away from me. At the time, I was young and I didn't know what to do. I didn't regret joining the Army, and maybe her decision was for the best, but I still hated Vanessa for not giving me the choice to make the decision, too.

Was Gabe right, though? Was I ready to settle down and start a family now? Was having Andi show up on my doorstep and giving me these thoughts a sign that it was time to leave the past in the past finally? Maybe Andi wasn't *the one*, but maybe she was the one who could remove the numbness from my heart.

When I pulled my *Jeep* into the garage, there was a white Acura on the right side of the driveway. It had no plates on the back of the car, but I'd bet my new roomie got new wheels because I hadn't seen the car earlier.

The water in Andi's shower was running and I groaned as I walked by on the way to my room to change, thinking about her under the hot water lathered with soap. I thought about the way it would cascade down from her shoulders to her thighs passing every place in between to rinse the suds off. How she would squirt shampoo into her hand and then work it into her damp hair, massaging her scalp and then turn and rinse it off. How she would do the same with the conditioner, but this time as the cream stayed in her hair, her hands would glide down to squeeze each tit then pinch her nipples until they puckered. She'd moan at the way it went straight to her pussy, turning her on as she'd think of me.

Her hand would travel from one of her breasts, making its way down her stomach to her coarse hair and slip between her legs. She'd throw her head back, leaving her body in the spray of the warm water and began teasing herself by applying pressure with the palm of her hand that stayed between her legs. Using the water with her arousal, she would start sliding her fingers through her needy pussy lips, making sure she took the time to massage her clit with her two fingers.

She'd groan out my name, wishing it was me using my fingers as she slipped one then two inside her, pumping in and out. She'd have to use the wall of her shower to brace herself from falling as she thrust over and over, bringing herself closer and closer to release. Knowing she was on the brink of exploding, she would take the hand holding herself up and widen her stance to brace herself as she slid her free hand down to viciously rub her clit causing her to moan. And then, as she came with a jerk, images of me would flash in her head because she'd want nothing more than to have me fucking her—hard.

Damn, I really needed to get laid!

After changing, I turned the corner to head to the kitchen and ran smack into a warm, wet, Andi. My dreams were coming true. "Gorgeous," I smirked. My arms wrapped around her, clutching the towel and preventing it from falling as hers went to my chest to steady herself.

"I, uh … I forgot my clothes in my room."

"Are you sure you didn't want me to see you naked?" I smirked.

A blush crept up her face. "No, I really forgot my clothes."

"Are you going to make this a habit?" It didn't go unnoticed that I was still holding onto her in the middle of our hallway.

She shook her head. "No, I have my first date tonight and I'm nervous."

"Why are you nervous? It's the same as D.C. isn't it?"

She paused. "I'm sure it is. I just wish it wasn't tonight. I needed more time to get situated."

"I know how you feel. I had my first date the day I moved to Vegas."

"Geez, they don't waste time."

"Gotta make that money, gorgeous."

She bit her bottom lip before responding and I had to fight every urge not to bend down and kiss her. She was naked in my arms and only a few inches from my lips. "Right. Well, I better get to it." She took a step back and I let go of the towel.

It dropped.

So did my gaze.

She hurried to pull up the towel as words spilled from her mouth. I assumed she sputtered words of embarrassment, but she had nothing to be embarrassed about. I wasn't listening to anything she was saying because I was focused on her. Her naked body was even better than what I'd imagined it to be. She was toned and lean; I could tell she took care of herself. I knew I was going to dream about her until she was mine. She *had* to be mine. The passion between us was there. I could feel it—almost taste it.

I grabbed her wrist lightly before she could retreat to her room, and cupped her face with my free hand. She tried to look down at the floor. "I know we just met, but there's nothing to be embarrassed about. You have a perfect body, Andi."

Her gaze met mine under hooded lids. "But that's the thing, we just met."

"You've never slept with one of your clients or had a one-night stand?" Her cognac eyes widened and I had my answer before she spoke. I took a step forward and brushed a strand of her hair out of her eyes. "Listen, gorgeous, I've been on plenty of dates with women and when I tell you that you have nothing to be ashamed of, I mean it. You're fucking perfect. So what if I caught a glimpse of you naked? I hope it's not the last time." I cracked a smile, hoping she'd follow my lead. She did and I breathed a sigh of relief. How in the world this shy chick went on dates for a living was beyond me.

"Are you wishing for naked Thursdays?" She laughed.

"Are you referring to the TV show *Friends*?"

She smirked and stepped out of my grasp. I watched as she walked toward the doorway of her room.

"You really are after my heart, gorgeous." I clenched my hands over my heart as if I were having a heart attack and backed up toward the kitchen.

She laughed, shaking her head as she closed herself in her room without another word.

I waited as long as I could for Andi to be ready for her date before I had to leave for mine. Not gonna lie, I wanted to see her dressed up. She walked down the hall in a simple dark blue dress and I immediately regretted my decision to wait. I was jealous. I knew, without a doubt, that I'd be thinking of her while I was on my date—which was a bad thing.

"Damn!" I said, dragging out the word. "What would you say if I was the one who bought you for the night?"

Her eyes lit up. "Did you?"

"I wish, gorgeous, I fucking wish. Whoever this guy is, he is one lucky motherfucker."

"I wouldn't make you pay for it." She grabbed her purse.

"Is that right?" I motioned for her to follow me to the garage so I could walk her out.

"I guess we'll see."

"We will. Oh, and Andi?" She turned to look at me. "Don't think about me too much on your date."

She laughed and got into her car. I noticed she always laughed and avoided me when I made references that probably made her uncomfortable. I still thought she was guarding something…

Maybe even hiding something.

Chapter Nine

Andi

"Don't think of me too much on your date."

Did Paul tell me that so I *would* think about him? Did he tell me that to keep my mind off of the fact that I was nervous as hell? Was he flirting? So many things were going through my mind as I drove to my *date.*

In the last forty-eight hours, I'd been in more compromising positions with Paul than I had been in with any other man in the last twelve years. The crazy thing was that I wasn't uncomfortable. I wasn't even running for the hills when his hands were on my ass in the hallway earlier as I stood dripping wet. I couldn't believe that I'd forgotten my clothes in my room or even my robe. I wasn't used to sharing a place with anyone and my mind was on the fact that I had a date *tonight.*

My date for the night was a dinner at Javier's in the Aria hotel. I had yet to be to the Strip, but the little I saw in the bumper to bumper traffic as I made my way to the hotel made me never want to go down there again. It was insane. It was almost better to get out and walk if I could, but I'd gotten a tip from Leah to valet park once I'd made it to the hotel. She assured me that all valet parking in Vegas was free, you'd just had to tip them when they got your car at the end.

After I valet parked and found my way to the restaurant, I took a deep breath and tried not to think about what I was actually doing. It reminded me of my seventeenth birthday. The circumstances were different, of course, but there was still a lot that was similar.

I was going on a *date*.

I was going on a date with a *stranger*.

And I was getting *paid*.

I needed to snap out of it. Be Andi, not Joss. I was undercover and no longer seventeen. I wasn't a scared little girl anymore. If anything were to happen, I had the training to protect me now. I would fight back.

I took a deep breath and walked into the dimly lit restaurant and up to the hostess stand. After telling her who I was meeting, she walked me to the table and my date stood as I approached.

"Andi," he greeted, kissing me on the cheek.

"Preston." I returned the kiss on his cheek.

Taking a long look at my date for the night, I decided this wouldn't be too bad. He was dressed in a pair of dark brown slacks and a black, long-sleeved shirt that hid what I imagined was a rock hard body. He had his sleeves rolled up a quarter of the way up his arms. *Why was that so damn sexy?* His blond hair was wrapped up into a man bun, and he had a strong jaw and beautiful blue eyes with a smile that gave off the impression—or maybe a warning—that he knew how to have a good time.

Taking my hand and guiding me to our booth he gave my body a once over with his eyes and smiled. "You, darlin', are absolutely gorgeous."

Gorgeous.

Flashes of Paul's smile danced across my mind. *"Don't think of me too much on your date."*

This was going to be a long night.

Doing my best to stay in character, I gave him what I hoped was a confident smile.

The night went on without a hitch. He was smart, sweet, and his smile didn't lie—he was a shit load of fun to be around. After dinner, Preston wanted to go dancing at Haze, the nightclub inside Aria. We stood in line for a few minutes, then once we got in, we went straight to the bar. He ordered a round of drinks, and I took in the atmosphere of the club as I waited for him to make his move.

I watched as people let loose all around me: grinding on each other, kissing, laughing and taking shots. They were living a carefree life, and I wondered what it would be like to let go and simply *be*. I'd never had that—*ever.*

Not wanting to ruin the good time I was having, and not wanting to fuck up my first date, I put a smile on face and turned my head back to Preston only to find him staring at me with *that* smile. He held a hand out to me. "Let's go, beautiful. I wanna show my date off."

Preston dragged me to the center of the dance floor and put an arm around my lower back, pulling me close. The first thing that hit my senses was the way he smelled, and I couldn't help but feel disappointed. Don't get me wrong, Preston smelled amazing, but his scent wasn't the one I craved.

"Don't think of me too much on your date."

Once again dragging my attention back to the man I was dancing with, I could feel the bass of the music through the soles of my feet vibrating all the way up to the top of my head. Between the beat of the music, the alcohol coursing through me, and the hard body I was dancing up against, I could feel my nerves starting to unwind. I was starting to let go for once, wanting to have what everyone around me had.

Turning in Preston's arms, I put my back to his front, and we started moving again. As soon as I closed my eyes, a pair of deep chocolate ones appeared in the forefront of my mind. When a pair of hands started making their way down my arms and grabbed my hips, it was no longer Preston I was dancing with—it was Paul. Throwing all inhibitions out the window, my hips started to really move with the music.

I was abruptly brought out of my fantasy by a pair of lips coming down to my ear with a deep baritone voice that I knew didn't belong to the man I was dancing with in my head. "Come up to my room with me."

Instantly I stilled and turned around. I had to think quickly; I didn't want him to notice the hesitation. "How about a few more drinks? I'm having so much fun and it's still really early."

For the rest of our date, I nursed the same drink with water on the side. In between the dancing and talking, I had him going back to the bar every chance I got. It was the only foolproof way I could think of to avoid the proposal of me going up to his room with him.

By the time our date was getting ready to wrap up, he could barely walk. The rest of the night went exactly as planned. I got Preston up to his room where he passed out on his bed and I was free and clear.

Maybe this whole escort thing wouldn't be so bad after all.

Chapter Ten

Paul

As I drove to my date's house, I thought about booking a date with Andi. It wasn't a bad idea. I mean, I shouldn't have to pay for one, but I would if it meant a date with her. But I didn't want the typical business-like first date. I wanted to hold her hand, kiss her, spend longer than two, three, four hours with her—I wanted the entire night. I wanted a real fucking date with her.

Instead, I was meeting a client. A client who was a regular. A client who wanted the boyfriend experience—the boyfriend experience at home that normally ended with me fucking her. I couldn't wait. The sooner I got laid, the sooner I'd be able to loosen up and get Andi out of my system.

When I arrived at Nikki's, I didn't bother to knock. Tonight I was her *boyfriend*. "Sugar?" I called out as I opened the door.

"I'm in the kitchen."

I rounded the corner and stopped dead in my tracks. Nikki was standing in the middle of her kitchen next to the granite countertop island, and she was butt-ass naked. In her hand was what looked like my drink of choice. I expected my dick to immediately go hard, but it didn't.

"You always know how to greet a man when he comes *home.*"

"Isn't this how a woman's supposed to treat her man?"

I chuckled and walked closer to her, kissing her *good,* then grabbed my drink. "Yeah, sugar, it is."

She slid onto the counter and spread her knees, clearly asking to be fucked right there. Normally, I would, but my cock wasn't even the slightest bit hard. Nikki didn't have the chestnut brown hair that I wanted to run my fingers through, she didn't have the whiskey brown eyes I wanted to get lost in, and there weren't specks of freckles dusting her cheeks.

Fuck …

I wanted Andi.

I only wanted Andi!

Not wanting to disappoint her, I took a few steps forward and stood between her knees. I ran my hands up her thighs until I could grab what I knew was a nice ass and pulled her forward until our hips met. Playing it up, I brought my lips within inches of her mouth and dropped my voice a couple octaves.

"As fucking tempting as you look right now, sugar, I was hoping I could have a relaxing night in with my girl. Maybe some take out and a movie." I was hoping she would take me up on my offer. She wanted a night in with dinner and a movie. I knew a movie led to sex and usually I would be all for it, but my dick wanted Andi…

And so did I.

I could smell the arousal coming from between Nikki's legs. Since this was a regular client and I needed her to keep rebooking and paying my bills, I thought of another solution as she batted her eyelashes and begged me.

"Please?"

"Don't move," I warned.

I went into her bedroom and searched the top drawer of her nightstand where I knew she kept her *toys*. We'd used them on several occasions. After I rummaged through and found the one I was looking for, I returned to the kitchen and found her exactly where I'd left her.

"Now, sugar, lean back."

She smiled and leaned back, her legs spread open and her pussy glistening. I didn't need the lube I'd grabbed from the nightstand, so I ran the tip of the clear glass dildo with the dark blue raised swirl that wrapped around the shaft into her juices.

Her back arched off the granite kitchen island as she moaned. "That feels so good."

"You like that, sugar?" I slipped the tip in a little, twisting.

She moaned her response and I twisted it further, rotating and following the blue swirl ridge. When the dildo was all the way in, I wasted no time and used it to fuck her—hard. It glided in and out effortlessly as she moaned, breathlessly. Usually, I would kiss her, grope her, ravish her. But this time, I leaned forward and spewed off a few dirty words about how she was making my dick hard or how hot she was as I grabbed her tit with my free hand. The only thing was, I had my eyes closed and instead of Nikki, all I thought about was Andi. She was the one I was whispering to. The one who I wanted naked in front of me, spread eagle, getting off on my words and my actions, but instead of a sex toy, it would be my dick fucking her.

Nikki's thighs clenched as she came, groaning and moaning my name. I knew it wasn't her best orgasm, and best was what I always wanted to deliver, so I flipped the dildo around. The other end had two balls at the end. The one closest to the shaft had small blue dots around the entire base giving it some texture and the other one at the very end was a little bit smaller, completely blue with a tip that was pointed just right so it would hit her G-spot.

"Holy fuck!" she cried.

"Now we're getting to the good stuff, sugar."

"You know what I like, daddy," she purred.

I shivered at the pet name she had for me. I hated it. Only children should call their father's daddy. Just like before, I thrust the glass rod in and out, twisting and turning. She started to buck so I knew she was close and I knew exactly what she needed to push her over the edge. Positioning the toy into the perfect position for direct stimulation to her G-spot, I lifted my free hand. Using her arousal to wet my fingers, I started strumming her clit.

"Oh God!" she shouted.

She thrashed and tried to close her thighs. Using my elbows, I kept her thighs apart as she shook and came, calling me God, then calling me Fucking God until she finally came down from her high and went limp, breathing heavy. I went to the sink to clean up as she caught her breath. When I turned around, I caught Nikki still in the same position staring at me, so I leaned against the sink counter, folded my arms and smirked as she started to speak.

"That was…"

"I know, sugar." I winked. Before she could say another word, I walked over and leaned in to give her shoulder a kiss. "Come on, go get cleaned up and into something comfortable. What do you want to eat? I'll order while you change and then we can pick a movie."

By the time I got home, Andi's car was in the driveway, but all the lights were off in the house and so was her bedroom light. I wasn't expecting her to be asleep. It was well before midnight and we'd both left for our dates at the same time, so I'd figured that we would come home at the same time, too. Something wasn't right. Maybe something had happened with her client.

I had a shower and then went to the kitchen to make something to eat, hoping that Andi would hear me rummaging around and come out—she didn't. I was really looking forward to spending more time with her. Damn, I was way over my head with this shit. I hadn't thought about a chick like this since *her*. Granted, I'd never lived with a woman (Autumn didn't count), so this was all new to me.

Mid-bite of my java chip ice cream, I saw a shadow out of the corner of my eye. I flicked my gaze from the TV and saw Andi walk into thc living room. I tried to hide my smile. She was dressed in pajama shorts that showed off her toned legs and a tight T-shirt. Yep, this female roommate thing was growing on me.

"Gorgeous," I greeted her.

"Hey," she sighed and sat next to me on the couch—but not close enough.

"Thought you were in bed or something."

She shook her head. "I was just unwinding from my date, checking on some things back in D.C."

"Everything okay?"

"Yeah," she yawned. "Jet lag catching up to me maybe?"

I draped my arm around her and pulled her closer. She didn't pull away. There was a reason she came out to be with me. "You can watch the *Tonight Show* with me. If you fall asleep, I'll put you to bed."

She smiled up at me. "Just wake me up if I do."

"Okay." I chuckled.

Not long after she was asleep. I fell asleep as well because I didn't want to wake her. I was a gentleman after all.

Chapter Eleven

Andi

A week had past and I was settling into the groove of things except I hadn't gone on any more dates. Mark got me business cards for S&R. They were sleek, shiny black cards with Andi Middlebrooke and my direct website link written on them. The cards were flashy and made me feel *official.*

But I needed more dates. I needed to do the job I was sent here to do. So I called Leah and Nina and they suggested I meet them at their favorite strip club.

"You have a date tonight?" Paul asked as I grabbed my keys from the kitchen table.

"No," I shook my head, "I'm meeting Leah and Nina." He eyed me up and down. "What?" I blushed.

"You're dressed as if you have a date."

"It's only a dress, Paul."

He stepped closer to me and I held my breath. The entire week I'd been avoiding him the best I could. I had a job to do and getting involved with him wasn't part of the job. Also, like everything else in my life, I was lying to him. Since my seventeenth birthday, I'd been lying to everyone. What was Paul going to do when he found out that I was really Joselyn? Would he still want me like he wanted me now?

"Gorgeous," he whispered against my neck as he moved my hair to the side. I tilted my head, allowing him to move as close to me as he could. "If you're going out to pick up a guy, you don't need to. I can be what you need."

I swallowed hard. "I'm going to get more clients. Gotta make that money." I repeated the words he'd once told me.

He chuckled and kissed my cheek. "When are you going to let me take you out?"

I couldn't deny the attraction I felt for him. I knew I had a curse, but luckily before it got to that point, my case would be over and I would be on my way back to D.C. "When are you going to ask me properly?" I teased.

He laughed again. "All right, gorgeous. Will you go out with me on Saturday?"

"I'll have to check my schedule."

"It's gonna be like that?"

I grabbed my keys and started to walk to the front door. "I'm just kidding, Paul James. Saturday works."

"Good, it's a date. I want you dressed like that." He waved his hand down the length of my body as I opened the door.

"I'll see what I can do."

As I closed the door, I heard him yell. "Hey! How do you know my middle name?"

Aw, fuck. I didn't realize I'd let that slip. I hurried to my car, turned it on and backed out of the driveway. He didn't try and follow me to question it further, thank God. Of course, I knew it from the FBI files and my research. I knew a lot about him. He grew up in Malibu, played football, got a full ride to UCLA but went into the Army instead, and then became a male escort. He'd never been in trouble with the law, he owned a self-defense business with his friends Gabe Hastings and Autumn Jones and I was updating it to add that he was dripping with sin.

The parking lot was packed when I arrived at the club. Unlike a week ago, I wasn't nervous as I got out of my car and walked to the glass door that was blacked out with a cellophane lining.

Usually, I arrived at a strip club dressed in pants, a comfortable shirt, boots and, more importantly, with my gun. This time, I had on a simple plum dress and black heels. Inside my clutch purse was my cell, money, driver's license, lip gloss, gum and my business cards—I felt naked to say the least.

After paying the cover, I entered the darkened room with neon lights and a disco ball. The bass of the music thumped as if it were a nightclub. There were several small round stages with polls running up to the ceiling and women dancing topless in front of men. In the back was a bigger stage where another dancer worked the crowd. She hung upside down, her legs spread and her tits dangling as men tossed money onto the stage.

I spotted Leah and Nina sitting at the farthest stage away from the door—as if they were scouting the place. They waved me over when they saw me and I smiled and walked over to them. We exchanged hugs in greeting.

"Come here often?" I joked.

"Every night." Leah laughed.

Nina waved at a waitress. "Let's get you a drink and then scope out the place. We just arrived, so we haven't had a good look."

I wasn't sure what I was really looking for other than a client. What I knew was clients came to us, not the other way around. We weren't prostitutes. We weren't selling *ourselves*, so I needed to follow their lead and not look like the narc that I was.

"I have to admit I've never picked up clients in a strip club." The waitress came over and I ordered a margarita.

Leah laughed. "That's not how they roll in D.C.?"

I smiled. "Well, not me, that's for sure."

"Was the president your client?" Nina asked.

I raised an eyebrow at her. "Do you think that if the president was my client that I would leave him to come to Vegas?"

"Wouldn't he just send his private jet?" Leah asked.

The cocktail waitress set our drinks down and I handed her my credit card, telling her that I was paying for all the drinks and to leave the tab open.

"You don't need to buy our drinks," Nina protested.

"President's money," I joked and we laughed. "But seriously, you think he'd spend the tax payer's money to send his private jet to pick up his escort for a date?"

They laughed. "No," Leah replied, "but we think he'd spend it to fly in so he could fuck her."

I choked on my drink. Did they all sleep with their clients? "The President is not my client," I exclaimed and left it at that. Somehow I needed to find out if they slept with their clients so I knew how to play my angle.

And then it hit me…

Did Paul sleep with his clients?

"I'll be right back." I needed a minute as I gathered my new thoughts on Paul. I didn't care if Leah and Nina slept with their clients. But Paul… The thought of him doing more than kissing one of his clients squeezed my heart.

Staring into the mirror, I took a deep breath.

"Are you okay?"

I turned to my left and saw that I wasn't the only one in the restroom. "I'm fine. Thank you."

"Are you here with your boyfriend?"

I smiled. "No, my friends." *Did girls come to strip clubs with their boyfriends?*

"Girls night out?" she asked, applying her scarlet lipstick. The red was a nice contrast to her light ebony skin tone and straight black hair.

"Something like that."

"You're not here with Leah and Nina are you?"

I tilted my head to the side slightly. "Yeah, do you know them?"

"Kinda. My boss has been trying to recruit them for years."

I raised my eyebrow. "Your boss? Who's your boss?"

She returned the cap on her lipstick then stuck it in her purse. "Mr. Martinez."

"What does he do?"

"You hang with those two and you don't know who he is?"

I leaned against the porcelain sink and crossed my arms. "I'm new in town."

"Oh, then you're perfect." She eyed me up and down with her brown eyes.

"Perfect for what?"

Before she could reply, the door opened and Leah walked in. She eyed the girl from head to toe, rolling her eyes as she turned to me. "Hey, are you okay? I came to check on you."

I smiled. "Yeah, I'm fine. I was just coming out." I smiled tightly at the mysterious girl.

I wanted to hand her my card because the way she talked about this Martinez guy had me intrigued. Maybe he recruited for another escort service, but I wanted to find out. Instead, I walked past her because I didn't want Leah to see my interest and made my way back to the table where we sat and watched topless women dance. The dancers couldn't be fully nude in Vegas if the establishment served alcohol.

"Who's Mr. Martinez?" I asked Leah and Nina as we scanned the floor.

Their eyes widened as they looked at each other and then they both answered in unison. "No one."

"What do you mean no one? Obviously he's someone."

"You don't want to get involved with him," Leah avowed.

"The girl…" I paused, realizing I never got her name. "The girl I met in the bathroom said I would be perfect for him."

"He's not a client," Nina said curtly.

I took a sip of my drink. "What is he?" I already knew he wasn't someone who paid for escorts, but I wanted to know *who* he was.

"Look, Andi," Leah begged, "just trust us. S&R is a good company to work for. Stick with them, okay? You don't want to get mixed up with Martinez and his crew."

I decided not to press her further on the subject tonight, but I was going to find out who this guy was. I'd do my own research in the FBI database if I had to.

"See anyone worth approaching?" Nina asked a few minutes later.

"How do I know?"

"Who's giving out the most money?"

I scanned the room. This was an upscale strip club. There were no three dollar cheeseburgers with two dollar shots, and no creepy dudes sitting in the front row in plain white T-shirts that only stared at the dancers and didn't give them any money. No, this place had decent looking guys giving a few dollars at a time.

I spotted a guy who kept looking over at our table. He was dressed in a suit, maybe in his early to mid-forties, and was sipping on a beer. If he was willing to give money to a dancer, then maybe he was willing to have a date with me—it was worth a shot.

"All right. I'm going in."

I took a final sip of my drink, stood and made my way to where he was sitting and took the chair next to him. He turned and smiled.

I smiled back. "Hi."

"Hi."

"Which girl is your favorite?"

He scanned the room and then his gaze landed on mine. "You."

I chuckled. "I'm not a dancer."

"No, but I bet you look good topless."

I held my tongue and kept flirting. "I don't go around flashing them."

"Is that right? What do I have to do to see them?" He turned his chair a little toward me.

"First you can start by buying me a drink." Before I could finish asking for one, a cocktail waitress placed it on the bar that wrapped around the mini stage. "Okay. I see how you work."

"Now what?"

I thought quickly as I took a sip of my margarita. "Are you from here?"

"On business."

"So you come here while your wife is at home with the kids."

He smiled and took a pull of his beer. "Something like that."

"Besides strip clubs, what else do you like to do in Vegas?"

"I like to try my luck at craps."

I took another sip of my drink, trying to sip as much as I could so I could leave. "I'm new in town and have only been to the Strip once and that was only for dinner and dancing. I haven't been on the casino floor yet."

"I'll need to take you then."

I reached inside my purse and grabbed my card then handed it to him. "I'd love that. Here's my card."

"Andi… Andi with an I." He smiled.

"And you are?"

"Derrick."

"Thank you for the drink, Derrick." I tipped the drink toward him and stood. "Contact me if you want company at the craps tables."

"I will, Andi with an I."

Approaching a potential client on my own wasn't that bad after all.

Chapter Twelve

Paul

Finally, it was Saturday night.

It felt as if I were still in high school, except in high school I'd had more confidence. Usually, I had a date on Saturdays with clients, but I'd made sure to have the day off. I wasn't worried about the money I'd miss out on. I was going to be with the most beautiful woman in Vegas. It was worth it.

All week it was hard to see Andi. It was almost as if we were dating, but we weren't. Every time I saw her, I wanted to kiss her. If we were dating, I could wrap her in my arms and kiss her whenever I wanted, but we weren't so I couldn't. I had to be a perfect gentleman when I saw her.

During the week, I'd had to leave a few times to go on a couple of dates, which felt awkward, but I hadn't had sex with any of the clients I went on dates with. It wasn't as if I could get in trouble for not having sex with clients. We weren't hired to sleep with them. We were hired for companionship. If things led to sex, then they led to sex. I, however, had my eye on my new roommate and I didn't want anyone else, so at the end of the date, I'd tell them I had a nice time and call it a night. I didn't even care if they re-booked anymore. Each time I thought about forgetting the escort thing. I didn't need it anymore. I had my new business with Gabe and Autumn and I was happy doing it. *Happier.* I felt alive now that Gabe and I were shooting again and teaching women how to defend themselves.

When I became an escort, it was my way to forget about Vanessa, but I no longer needed to forget about *her* and what she'd done. I was ready to move on. Even if Andi and I just went out for the night, it was a step in the right direction.

While Andi got ready in her room, I showered then changed into a pair of dark denim jeans and a black button-down shirt. After combing my hair back, I rolled up my long sleeves and went out to the living room where I waited for her to be ready. When she came out, I wanted to tell her how good she looked in her tight jeans and sparkly top. How good she smelled as she stepped closer to me. How fucking perfect she was.

But I had a plan.

"I'll pick you up at seven." I grabbed my keys, my wallet, and my cell phone and started to walk toward the garage.

"Um, it's 6:55 now."

"Seven o'clock, gorgeous." I closed the door to the house from the garage before she could respond. After starting up my *Jeep*, I backed it out of the garage, drove around the block and stopped in front of our house so I could pick her up for a proper date.

At seven o'clock sharp I stepped out of the *Jeep* and walked to the front door. I knocked and waited for Andi to open the door. She smiled brightly when she answered it.

"Damn," I said, dragging out the word. "Gorgeous, you're stunning."

She looked down at herself and then back up to my eyes. "Thank you."

I reached out my hand. "Ready?"

"Is it seven?"

I narrowed my eyes at her. "You're lucky I love your feisty mouth." She blushed and grabbed my hand. "You're cute when you blush."

"Let's go, Paul," she groaned and I laughed. This was going to be fun and I couldn't wait.

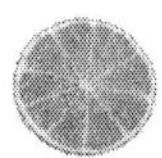

"Are you going to tell me where we're going?" Andi asked, breaking the silence. We'd barely driven out of our neighborhood.

"How do you feel about heights?"

Her eyes became huge. "Seriously?" I nodded and returned my gaze to the road. "What if I say I don't like them?"

I shrugged and glanced at her. "Too bad."

"Paul!"

"Are you scared of them?" I chuckled.

"I'm deathly afraid of them."

"Aw, gorgeous, you have me. I won't let anything happen to you."

"You can't save me from falling to my death."

I grabbed her hand and looked into her eyes as we stopped at a red light. "We're not going to fall to our death. Trust me."

"I trust you. It's whatever's in the sky I don't trust. Which is …?"

"The world's largest observation wheel."

"The Ferris wheel on the Strip?"

"It's not a Ferris wheel." I laughed, shaking my head. "Each pod's enclosed and can hold up to forty people. Worse case, you can go to the middle and not look down."

"I don't know about this, Paul."

I squeezed her hand. "We're going to dinner at The LINQ first. You have time to prepare. If you really don't want to do it when we get there, you don't have to. But I promise it's not that bad. Plus it's the best view of Vegas, especially at night."

She groaned and turned her head to look at the window and I smiled. She was going to go up on the High Roller even if I had to carry her. I could have taken Andi to any number of nice restaurants on the Strip, but we were wined and dined all the time, so I wanted to take her somewhere casual. I wanted to show her Vegas and not have to drive out of town to see the view.

After valet parking, I grabbed Andi's hand and led her through the casino to the restaurant where we were going to eat. I was starting to get used to having her hand in mine. It felt like a natural thing for us to be doing. Maybe it was because the casino was crowded and it was easier for her to follow me. I didn't care. I loved the feel of her skin, and if I needed to enforce a death grip, I would.

A few minutes into our walk through the casino, Andi turned her head to me. "First you told me to dress up and then you changed your mind and told me to dress casually." It was as if she'd just remembered

I said we were going to dinner and not only to The High Roller.

I smiled. "I know."

"Where are we going to eat then?"

"Why do you always ask so many questions?" We stepped around a group of rowdy drunks trying to decide where to go or something.

"I always know the plan before I do things."

"Even on personal dates?" She nodded and I stared at her for a beat, trying not to run into people as we walked and then I glanced up. "We're here."

"Guy Fieri's restaurant?"

"Do you watch the *Food Network*?"

"Sometimes." She licked her lips and I groaned.

"Hungry?"

"Starving."

We waited twenty minutes at Guy Fieri's Vegas Kitchen & Bar to be seated in the rustic bar type restaurant. I chose the place because the High Roller was only about a five minute walk outside the doors. Once we left, Andi could look at the wheel and make her final decision. It was 550 feet tall and took thirty minutes to make a full turn. I knew I could talk her into doing it for thirty minutes, even if I had to wrap her in my arms the entire time.

"Do you always order a margarita?" I asked her after the waiter left from taking our order.

"I'm not much of a drinker, but you can get a lot of different flavors with margaritas and tequila. How about you, what's your poison? I see you ordered tequila, too."

"That's true. I've always been a tequila man myself, especially when I can lick it off of *you.*" I smirked.

She laughed, placing her hand over her stomach. "Wow… Okay. How often do you use that line?"

The waiter came back and placed our drinks down. "I've never used the line on someone before. Body shots just happen." I winked at her before I took a sip of my tequila and coke.

"You might have to show me that talent one day." I choked a little on my drink but before I could respond she asked, "So how long have you been in the business?"

I wasn't sure why she'd changed the subject. I liked the flirty Andi, and I wanted to lick tequila and salt off of every inch of her, but I didn't press her on the matter. Instead, I answered her question with a sigh. "Long enough."

"You sound like you don't enjoy it."

Looking into the eyes of the woman asking me the question felt like a million light bulbs going off. I wanted to tell her how I felt about her, but it was hard because I didn't know how she felt about me. I really liked her. I wanted to see where things could go between us since we lived together. I didn't want it to be awkward at all. I'd already gotten my heart broken once and I was ready to move on with my life, but I wasn't sure I was ready to tell a woman I was ready to move on with her. I wanted to get to know her—in more ways than one, but was I ready to actually quit S&R?

"I'm starting to realize I want more out of life."

"You've never been in a serious relationship before?"

I sighed then took a long sip of my drink, contemplating if I wanted to tell her about Vanessa. After a few seconds, I realized that getting into a deep conversation about Vanessa wasn't something I wanted to do on a first date even if Andi and I lived together. If we did want to give whatever *this* was between us a chance, then maybe I would eventually tell her that I was in love once. *Everyone* had been in love before.

"It's been a long time, gorgeous. A really long time."

Before she could ask me to elaborate on the subject, the waiter dropped off our food and the subject was changed—thank God. We ate our food for a bit and then we picked up on more of the conversation.

"How are you liking Vegas?" I asked moments later after we'd gushed about how delicious the food was.

"It's definitely different. D.C.'s nothing like it is here."

I smiled behind my straw. "I heard through the grapevine that you're going to titty bars with some of the girls. You into girls, too?"

She snorted as she tried to contain her laughter. "Definitely not. The girls claim it's a good way to pick up clients, and seeing as I'm new to the area, I guess I'm trying to pull whatever tricks are out there."

"So you're not out there having threesomes with your clients and the girls?" My smile hadn't faltered as I thought about Andi with another chick.

"I've never slept with *any* of my clients. Do… Have you?" Her gaze avoided mine as she waited for my answer.

Would she not want to be with me because of something I'd done before I met her? I took another long sip of my tequila and coke, slurping the remaining content. "Honestly, gorgeous, I have. I have with a lot of them. But since you barged into my house—literally—I haven't. I haven't wanted to. I've been looking forward to this date since before I knew I wanted to take you on it, and hearing that you don't sleep with your clients... Fuck, that makes me so happy. You have no fucking idea how much that makes me happy."

Before we could continue, the waiter came and dropped off the check. "We can talk about this later. Let's go check out the High Roller."

"What if I freak out?"

"I'll wrap you in my arms until it's over."

She stared up at the metal wheel. "It's so high."

"Look how big the pods are. Nothing's going to happen. We'll stand in the middle if you're scared."

She tore her gaze to mine. "Promise?"

I smiled and grabbed her hand, missing the contact that was only brief from me paying for our tickets. "I promise, gorgeous."

We waited in line to enter onto the white pod. Occasionally the wheel would change colors from pink to green to blue and so on. Earlier I thought I would be the one that needed to have the death grip on Andi's hand, but she was the one that had one on mine.

"Don't worry, it's going to be okay," I promised, pulling her closer to me. I got a whiff of her hair and I noticed that she smelled of coconuts. "You smell like paradise."

She looked up at me. "Are you trying to distract me?"

I smirked. "Is it working?"

"Maybe a little." She looked back up at the wheel and I shook my head. I didn't get the heights thing. Maybe it was because I was used to helicopters in the Army and that shit didn't even have doors on it.

The line moved and it was our turn to enter the pod. Andi glanced at me and I whispered that it was going to be okay and I gave her hand a final squeeze. I saw her chest rise and then she entered and went straight to the center of the ball while everyone else went to the glass walls. I walked up behind her, wrapped my arms around her and pulled her to my chest, not saying anything while she took in her surroundings.

"Okay," I heard her say after a few minutes.

"Okay?" I questioned.

She nodded and started to step toward the glass, her hand in mine. Just before we got to the railing, she stopped and looked down.

"Gorgeous," I laughed, "you're not supposed to look down."

She looked up at me. "I wanted to see how far up we were."

"Well, shit. You're lucky we aren't all the way on top yet."

"I know." She stepped as close as she could to me, our shoulders pressed together, our hands still clasps and then she took the tiny step forward to the railing.

We were silent again as the wheel took the slow turn. The lights lit up the dark Vegas sky. Each casino could be seen below, and I wanted to point everything out to her, but I kept my mouth shut and let her take everything in. The closer we inched up to the top, the tighter her hand held mine.

I needed to distract her.

I tugged on her hand so she would turn her head to me, and when she did, I leaned down and captured her lips with mine. I wrapped the hand I was holding around my waist and let go so I could reach up and grab her face with both of my hands. Her other arm wrapped around my side as I finally got a taste of my girl.

Everyone in the pod disappeared. It was just her and me. I wanted her to only focus on me, so I stepped closer, pressing her back against the glass. The taste of tequila was faint when I swiped my tongue against her lower lip wanting her to open for me. When she finally granted me access and our tongues collided, there was a little grain of salt left over from her drink and the combination of the two only drove my need to really be with her.

I pushed against her a little harder, causing one of my knees to go between her legs. Our mouths worked together, tasting, sucking and not caring if others were watching. Really I couldn't give a fuck because this was what I'd been craving for the last two weeks and getting this little taste of her was only going to drive my need for her that much more. I wanted to taste every fucking inch of her.

As I was about to whisper into her ear that I couldn't wait to get her home to fuck her brains out, she quickly brought her hands up to cover mine that were holding her face and broke the kiss. She pulled her lips away and we kept our foreheads connected. Frustrated, I closed my eyes panting.

"Andi…"

Chapter Thirteen

Andi

Never in my wildest dreams would I have thought I would know what it was like to date *two* guys at once. Theoretically, I wasn't. I was only dating Paul. I was also dating other men. But I was only dating Paul for real.

Holy shit, I was *only* dating Paul!

When I accepted the assignment to come to Vegas, I never thought that I'd start dating someone. Dating was not on my radar.

Even though I stopped our kiss the night on the High Roller, it wasn't because I didn't want to keep going; it was because I was in my head. That was what I did when it came to all guys I tried to date. It was my curse. My mother, Tony, and Marco had cursed me the night of my seventeenth birthday. I wanted to be normal, to forget about how they ruined me, but no matter what I did, I was reliving that night.

The situation was weird, though. Paul and I lived together so we saw each other all the time. It was as if our relationship was progressing faster than normal and I couldn't have that. I was freaking out. *Literally freaking the fuck out.* I hadn't had sex in twelve years and he'd had sex yesterday—okay not yesterday, but close enough. How was I going to dodge that bullet and still live with him while I did my investigation? Did I want to dodge that bullet? What if I told Paul the truth?

This wasn't part of the plan.

Paul wasn't part of the plan.

It had been a few days since our date and things were good—really good. I knew sex was coming.

The sex was coming.

Rolling out of bed, I tossed my hair into a messy bun and went to the kitchen for coffee. Paul was shirtless like always, and I bit my lower lip to hide my smile as he turned. I wanted to smile, but it would only feed his ego and we had our little banter I'd grown accustomed to.

He grabbed my wrist and tugged me to him before I reached the coffeemaker. "Don't think I didn't see that, gorgeous."

"See what?" I peered into his chestnut colored eyes.

"I know you're hot for my body." He nipped at my ear and it sent a tingle down my belly. I stifled a moan.

Yeah, I was hot for his body.

Drip.

Drip.

Drip.

"You think so?" I joked as I tilted my head and allowed him to kiss my neck.

He worked his way up to my mouth. "Shut up and kiss me, woman."

And I did.

My hands wrapped around his neck and his arms wrapped around my waist as our lips locked. The taste of coffee lingered when our tongues got their first taste of each other this morning. I wasn't going to lie. I could get used to this.

"Remind me to thank Mark again for moving you into my house," he murmured against my lips then kissed me again, our tongues savoring the feel of how lucky we were.

I smiled against his lips. "I thought I just barged in here?"

He pulled back. "You're feisty even without coffee." He slapped my ass playfully as I walked to the coffee pot and poured myself a cup. Little did he know I'd been awake for half an hour preparing myself because today was day three after our date and if you thought about it, it could be date number three. Guys always wanted sex on or before date three. I didn't know what to expect except …

The sex was coming.

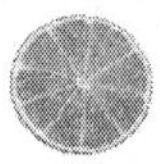

Even though I had no update, I called the secure line for the bureau and gave an update. I told them briefly about how the girl in the bathroom had mentioned Mr. Martinez and how I was going to investigate him further.

As far as Paul, we came up with rules for working even though we'd just started dating. When we went to work, we were only allowed to go to dinner, Vegas shows, or be a *lucky charm* at a casino for someone. We could hold their hands with minimal kissing, but no getting naked (that was for him). If things got to a certain point where we might not be able to stop a client from getting mad because they wanted more from us, then we ended the date. I wasn't too worried about that; I had done more research and learned that most companies have a policy that female companions weren't *allowed* in client rooms—at least that would be my excuse.

As far as the sex…

We'd passed day six of dating and no sex. I wasn't sure I could do the sex anyway. I wanted to do the sex. I really did, but it was a mind over matter thing.

And I was scared.

Luckily, Paul was busy with dates at night and during the day he had his self-defense classes with Gabe so we had minimal interaction. He did, however, mention he wanted me to meet his friends, and that was a big step. I needed to see where this was all going before I brought more people into the mix because I was certain I was leaving after the investigation was over.

Dates were starting to book through my website and tonight was my first date since the one I had when I first arrived. It happened to be with Derrick from the strip club. He was back in town and wanted to try his luck at the craps table. I had no idea how to play craps, but like everything else, I was going to fake it.

After checking my back office and the details for my date with Derrick, I walked into the kitchen and stopped and eyed what Paul was doing then asked. "Whatcha doin'?"

He placed a few more items into a backpack. "Packing for our date."

"Our date?" I asked, confused.

"Yep."

"When are we going on a date?"

"Now."

"Seriously?"

"I don't joke about dates."

I looked at what he was wearing. "Do I need to change?" I was wearing jean shorts and a tank top and he was in basketball shorts and nothing else.

He stopped stuffing the bag and turned to me. "Just your shoes actually. Or maybe something you'd wear to the gym."

I raised an eyebrow. "We're going to the gym?"

"Nope."

"Are you going to tell me what we're doing?"

He turned and caged me against the countertop. "Well, I'm going to get you all sweaty and then feed you."

I laughed. "Why are you being so vague?"

"You know I like to fuck around." He took my lips, silencing me for a few seconds.

"Fine, don't tell me. Will we be back in time for my date tonight?" The sentence sounded weird as it rolled off my tongue.

"Of course, gorgeous."

I changed and so did Paul and then we jumped in his *Jeep*. I hated not knowing the plan when it came to things—anything. I was a planner.

"Where are we going?" I asked again as we drove farther out of town.

He looked over at me and smirked. "Oh right, I forgot. You can't go with the flow."

I stuck my tongue out at him.

"Lean that closer over to me."

I did as he asked and we kissed briefly and then he returned his attention back to the road. We drove some more and then finally turned down another road.

"We're going to Mount Charleston?" I asked as I read the sign.

"Yep."

"To…?"

He chuckled. "Hike."

"Oh." I smiled. I could do that. It beat going to the smoky casinos and since we were driving for a while, I knew we weren't going to a gym.

"That's the sweaty part and then we'll have a picnic."

"I can handle that."

He squeezed my hand that he was already holding and he smiled.

Drip

Drip

Drip

I clenched my thighs trying to relieve the ache building between them. No matter how much I wanted to deny it, I wanted this sinful man beside me.

We hiked a five and a half mile trail that looped around. I followed Paul because I had no idea where I was going even though it was pretty much one way and was clearly marked. I was enjoying being outdoors, taking in the scenery; the vast mountains, lush trees and when we started hiking, the sky was blue with only a few white clouds. By the time we were heading back, a few darker clouds had started to roll in.

"I think it's going to rain." I looked up at the sky.

"We'll be fine." I gave him a questioning look. "It's only a few clouds."

We found an empty patch of grass and Paul opened his backpack. He pulled out a thin, plush blanket just big enough for the both of us. I expected him to pull champagne from his backpack, but instead he had sandwiches, fruit, chips, and water packed. He even had a cookie for each of us.

"Thanks for lunch," I said, breaking off a piece of the cookie.

He was laying on his side with his elbow under him for support when he leaned in and took my lips. It tasted of the chocolate from the chocolate chip cookie. "I really like spending time with you, Andi."

My face heated despite the chill that was starting to move in with the clouds. "I like spending time with you too."

"Tell me about your life before moving to Sin City."

I tensed briefly, trying to stare him in the eyes so he didn't know I was about to lie to him. "You know, dates and stuff." I shrugged as if it was no big deal since it was what we did here.

He chuckled. "No, gorgeous, besides working."

Well, shit. All I did was work, even if it wasn't escorting. I shrugged again as I took another piece of the cookie. "Normal girl stuff like manis, pedis, getting my hair done." Really I did none of that stuff. I occasionally treated myself to a pedicure and I, of course, got my haircut. But I didn't care. I didn't care about any of it.

"Why did you move to Vegas?"

"I'd heard escorts made more money here, so I wanted to give it a shot." Luckily I was prepared for that question. It really didn't make any sense for me to move to Vegas without any friends or family here.

"Friends?"

I decided to tell him the truth. "My best friend is a guy who I've known my entire life. My other best friend, Catherine, lives in Florida and I see her maybe once a year."

"Why is that?"

I sighed. "We're just too busy and don't plan anything since we don't live in the same state."

"I guess I can see that, but your job allows you to make your own schedule."

Shit! "Not Cat's. She works as a dental assistant and I'm not really sure how her vacation works, but we don't plan vacations. Sometimes she comes up to see Seth and I. You're right, though, we definitely need a girl's trip. I'm just not a big flyer."

"You're scared to fly?"

"Not scared really. Just only flown a few times."

Paul sat up and reached over, tucking a strand of my hair behind my ear. "Well, anyone who doesn't take the time to spend even a minute with you, is crazy."

The way he looked at me caused my insides to flip flop. In a simple look, he made me feel as though I was the only girl who existed.

He made me feel wanted.

Needed.

Cared for.

They say the eyes are windows to the soul and Paul's eyes gave him away. There was something there. Deep. He came off as a smart ass, sexy as sin escort who did everything on a whim because he could; never wanting to settle down and having too much fun. But I could see right through him. I saw the way he looked at the older couples on our date and felt him hold my hand that much tighter.

Paul Jackson could easily be my forever.

I cleared my throat to keep myself from attacking his lips. I was loving my time with him, and I didn't want it to end too soon. "Okay, your turn. Tell me something about yourself I don't know. Past. Present. Future. I don't care." It was silly. I had done such extensive research on him, there was not much he could tell me I didn't already know.

Looking up to the darkening clouds as in deep thought for just a few moments he looked at me and shrugged, "I don't like Brussel sprouts."

Laughing, I went to playfully punch his shoulder for being a smart ass, but when my fist connected with his shoulder, he grabbed it and yanked me toward him. He fell to his back, pulling me down so I was laying on top of him. Just that fast, the air around us went dense.

I couldn't breathe.

Using both hands to swipe the loose hair from my ponytail, he paused and cupped my face with both hands. "Who *are* you, Andi?" he whispered. "How has some lucky bastard not swept you off your feet yet?"

I took my first full, deep breath in what felt like way too long and smiled. "I'm just me."

When he didn't smile back but continued to look at me as if he was seriously trying to answer his own question, the butterflies in my stomach started up again. Doing the only thing physically possible—because I knew I wouldn't be able to speak a single word—I brought my lips to his.

This kiss wasn't rushed. It wasn't wild as if we were trying to satisfy a craving we were both fixing for. This connection was slow and passionate. This was one of those moments little girls watch in movies, hoping and praying they will experience it at least once in their lifetime just to feel that connection with another person.

The more I got to really know Paul, the more he was chipping away at my resolve. I didn't come here with the intention of getting into any kind of relationship, but he was slowly working his way in…

And I loved it.

Paul sat us up with my knees straddling his hips and softly ran his lips over mine before I advanced again. It was as if my mouth was designed for his. I parted my lips, inviting the invasion of his tongue. He swept one hand to the back of my neck, deepening the kiss while the other hand traveled down and wrapped around my lower back to hold me tighter.

As though someone had flipped a switch, the sky opened up and started pouring. On instinct, I started to stand and make a beeline for the nearest cover, but before I could lift myself up, he grabbed my arm and stilled me.

"Wait..." He was wearing his usual devious smile.

Being in this moment with him I felt happy and free. Like I didn't have a care in the world. It was just us—Andi and Paul—enjoying the here and now, and I didn't want it to end.

I tipped my head back feeling the rain on my face and spread my arms out to the sides. Paul's hands gripped my hips, making their way around my waist. I looked back down at him and laughed. Needing to touch him, I brought my hands back and ran them through his finger length brown hair. He dipped his head, resting against my chest and in response, I simply wrapped my arms around him. I knew what he was saying without him speaking a single word. I felt it too.

And it scared the hell out of me.

"Should I be jealous?" Paul asked as I came into the living room dressed for my date.

I looked down at my fire engine red dress. "It's not my fault you told me to dress casually for our two dates."

He pulled me down so I was straddling him on the couch and it caused me to squeal. "But I'm the lucky one who gets to see you in your pajamas."

I smiled and leaned forward to kiss him briefly. "Exactly and you're gonna make me late."

"Where are you going?"

"The Palazzo to play craps."

"Do you know how to play?"

I shook my head and laughed. "Do I even need to know how to play?"

"Not looking like this." He laughed and ran his hands up both of my bare thighs until they rested on my ass. Goosebumps pricked my skin and that butterfly feeling returned to the pit of my stomach.

Drip.

Drip.

Drip.

"Well, I'm going to wing it, blow on the dice, flirt." I shrugged.

He groaned. "Yeah, this whole dating other people thing isn't working."

"How do you think I felt all week?"

He leaned his head back on the couch, looking up at the ceiling, but not removing his hands from my butt. "I never thought I was a jealous man before you."

"I thought you didn't date before me?"

He raised his head just enough so his gaze could meet mine. "No, I said I hadn't been in a serious relationship in a long time."

I smirked. "So we're in a serious relationship?"

The grip on my ass tightened and he moved in one swift motion so I was laying on the couch and he was hovering over me, one leg on the floor. "Yeah, gorgeous, we are."

"I'm kidding, sugar lips."

"Sugar lips?" He grinned.

"You don't like it?"

"I've upgraded to a nickname?"

I nodded.

"I guess it could be worse." He paused for a beat. "Dingleberry."

I laughed—hard. My stomach clenching and tears pricking my eyes. If I didn't stop, I would have to fix my makeup and for sure be late for my date. "Dingleberry?" I finally said, still with laughter in my voice.

"Do you know what a dingleberry is?"

I chuckled again at the visual. "I do, and if you want me to call you a turd, I will."

He kissed my lips. "Sugar lips is better."

"Good. Now I'm really going to be late." I pushed on his chest so he'd let me off the couch.

He kissed me one last time.

When I was walking out the door, he yelled, "Are you sure you don't want to blow me for luck first?"

After valet parking, I walked into the Palazzo and found my way to the LAVO Lounge where I was meeting Derrick. My back office instructions said that he would be waiting for me before we hit the tables. The LAVO Lounge has a bar and restaurant on one side and a nightclub on the other. I'd been told it could get pretty steamy on the dance floor.

When I entered the swanky, dimly lit bar, I scanned it for Derrick.

The lounge could be described as a modern day speakeasy with deep crimson plush furnishings, rich woods throughout, and high back chairs to make any man feel like a king. I spotted Derrick sitting at the bar, dressed in a pair of dark slacks and a charcoal grey button-down shirt with the sleeves rolled up to the elbows. He was definitely easy on the eyes and I questioned why he would hire an escort. He'd mentioned he had a wife at home.

He turned and smiled. "Andi with an I." He stood and I leaned in to kiss his cheek.

"Hello, sweetie."

"Baby girl, I'm anything but sweet."

"Is that right?"

He winked. "Maybe you'll find out." I laughed, ignoring the innuendo. "Margarita again?" He nodded to his drink and that's when I saw his forearm and the dragon tattoo sticking out of the rolled up sleeve.

In his suit, Derrick looked like a well-dressed business man, but underneath I would bet he was tatted up. Not everyone is who they appear to be. Some people will do anything to appear to be the perfect person on the outside.

"Yes, on the rocks with salt please."

"I remember." He nodded to the bartender.

I sat in the empty chair and waited for my drink. "So, what kind of business are you in town for?"

With a straight face he answered, "Porn."

I laughed. "Well, we are in Vegas after all, but I wasn't expecting that answer. What are you an actor?" I glanced down at his tattoo and then back up to his eyes.

His gaze followed mine and he laughed. "No, I'm only kidding. I'm a salesman trying to get our shit in every hotel on the Strip."

The bartender placed my drink in front of me and I took a sip. "What kind of shit?"

"The toiletries in the hotel rooms."

"Really? That's cool."

"Not really." He laughed and took a pull of his beer. "But I don't want to talk about work, Andi with an I." He grabbed a piece of my long dark brown hair, twirling the end then releasing it.

I smiled. "Other than strip clubs, what's a man like you do for fun in Sin City?"

"I only gamble with a lucky charm because I always lose, and I hate going to the corny shows by myself, so I just like to look at tits and ass." His gaze roamed up and down my legs then rested on my boobs before finally my eyes as he waited for my response.

I grabbed my drink, took the final sips and stood, ready to get the show on the road.

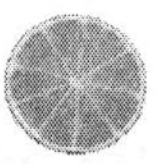

The cheers of people could be heard all around us as we walked toward the tables of the Palazzo. People smoked cigarettes, drank and bumped into us—basically it was your typical Saturday night in Vegas.

"Do you know how to play?" Derrick asked as we got closer. His hand was in mine, but it felt weird. It wasn't Paul's and I missed him. I missed his smell, his touch, his laugh, his voice, and it hadn't even been two hours. It was probably because I was out with another man. Yeah, this whole dating other people thing sucked, but I had no leads on the sex trafficking situation and I had to keep going until I did.

I shook my head. "I'm more of a blackjack girl."

"Let's try craps and see what happens. I want to see your mouth blow something."

My gaze darted to his. "I'm good at that." I really wasn't. I'd never given a blowjob a day in my life. We could thank the curse for that.

He groaned as we stepped up to the table. "I bet you are, baby girl. Damn … I bet you are."

I smiled up at him and waited for him to place his bet, but he didn't. "Why aren't you placing a bet?" I whispered.

He wrapped his arm around my shoulder and pulled me closer to him. "I'm waiting to become the shooter." He kissed the top of my head. I nodded as if I knew what that meant—I had no idea.

The cocktail waitress came over and we both ordered drinks. Finally, Derrick placed a bet on the pass line. I couldn't tell how much, but the table had a minimum of twenty dollars per bet. He was passed the dice and then he reached out for me to blow on them. I leaned forward and blew.

When I looked up, all eyes were on me and I smiled, wondering if they thought I was his girlfriend or his mistress—I guess I kinda was both. When I continued to scan the table, my gaze fell on familiar brown ones. I tilted my head in question and she waved.

"What are you doing here?" I mouthed. She didn't say anything as she started to walk toward me.

Derrick turned to me and said, "Our number is eight."

"What does that mean?"

"We rolled an eight. We can't roll an eight or our turn is over."

"How do we win money?"

He was already reaching to place chips down on the ten. "We have to roll a ten now, Andi with an I." He held up his hand with the dice and I blew. He rolled a three.

I frowned. "Aw, I'm sorry."

"It's not an eight." He laughed.

"We keep going?"

He nodded and placed more chips on the two on the green felt table and I looked over at the girl from the strip club that told me about Mr. Martinez. She was standing next to me, waiting for me to acknowledge her, but Derrick was in the middle of betting. He reached out again with the dice for me to blow on and I did. He tossed them on the table.

"Yes!" I cheered as I counted the two die; he'd rolled snake eyes. He hugged me then grabbed his winnings and the dice. "More?" I asked.

"We go until we roll an eight." He chuckled.

"Oh," I stammered and turned quickly to the chick next to me. "What are you doing here?" I whispered again.

"I saw you over here and wanted to come say hi."

"I'm working."

"I know."

Derrick turned to me and I smiled up and him and blew. I wasn't sure which number he placed a bet on; I just hoped he won.

"Let's talk after your date is over," she continued.

I wanted to tell her to fuck off because I wanted to go straight home to Paul, but I was here to do a job both for S&R and the FBI. I nodded. "Yeah. I'll meet you at the valet at midnight."

Cheers erupted around the table. Derrick turned and we hugged. He must have won. When he turned to grab the dice, the girl was gone.

"Pick a number, baby girl," Derrick offered, holding chips out to place a bet.

I looked at the table, leaned closer and then back to him. "Five."

"If I roll a five, you have to kiss me."

I smiled. "Okay." I blew on the dice again and sure enough he threw a five. Without hesitation, I stood and wrapped my arms around his neck, planting my lips on his. It was nothing like kissing Paul. I felt nothing. There were no butterflies in my stomach, no drip in my panties, nothing.

I blew on the dice again and he threw an eight, the crowd groaned and he drew me to him.

"What does that mean again?"

"We lost and my turn is over."

"Aw man."

"I won a grand, though," he beamed, riffling his chips.

"So I *am* your lucky charm?"

He pulled me to him and kissed me again. "Yeah, you sure are."

We stayed at the table while he placed bets on other shooters until he was the shooter a few more times. Twice he won on the come out roll. I was starting to believe I was really his lucky charm because he was racking in the dough.

The date was coming to an end and I was walking him toward the elevators where I was going to say goodbye.

"Come up to my room with me, Andi with an I." His arms wrapped around my waist, his body flush with mine as he leaned into me and against the waiting elevator wall.

"Sweetie, you know I can't do that."

"I'll pay extra," he whispered into my ear.

"Let's not ruin a good thing."

He pulled his head back and stared into my eyes. "What do you mean?"

"You just won a lot of money. Go call your wife."

"Right. I paid for a hooker and I can't even get laid. Just like at home."

"Derrick, I'm not a hooker. There's a difference."

He jabbed his finger repeatedly for the elevator. "Just go."

"I'm sorry."

My heart broke a little as I walked away and he got into the elevator. I turned slightly and saw his head hung low as the doors closed. I wanted to run back and hug him. Even though he was a client, I'd had a really good time with him. I had no interest in him romantically, but I could tell he was a good guy. I'd thought for sure he'd hired me because he slept around on his wife, not because his wife wasn't sleeping with him at home.

Like his hidden tattoo, you never knew what people were hiding.

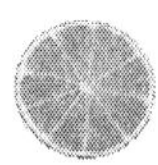

When I made it out to valet, it had slipped my mind that Martinez's girl would be waiting for me, but sure enough she was. She was sitting on a bench, smoking a cigarette and staring at her cell phone as I approached her.

I slid in beside her. "I didn't think you'd come," she remarked blowing smoke above our heads.

"Had to come get my car."

"Where did you want to go to talk?"

"We can talk right here," I suggested.

"Suit yourself. Are you enjoying your time here, honey?"

"It's Vegas. How could you not?" I gave a nervous laugh.

She laughed, too. "You still haven't seen the half of it. You're going to be a fun cherry to pop. Let's not beat around the bush here."

"Andi. And you are?"

"Jasmine." She reached out her hand and we shook like we were having a business meeting. Maybe we were. "Listen, Andi, what if I told you I could triple what you make on one of your pathetic, boring dates?"

I laughed, my eyebrows scrunching. "Who said my dates are boring? I just had a great time at the craps table."

"Oh come on, Andi. I know girls like you. Every girl wants a little more *fun.* Besides, you're missing the bigger picture here. I'm talking about a very comfortable income, plus some extracurricular *activities.* Listen, before you say anything," she continued, "I've spoken with my boss about you. Someone with your innocence could be *beneficial*." Her gaze roamed my bare legs and I felt violated. "Here's my card. When you're ready for a little more excitement, you know how to reach me."

I reached for her card and our fingers brushed. Hers lingered, and I wanted to pull mine away but didn't. I kept them there as long as she wanted because I was playing the part of Andi, not Joss.

"How do you know I'm innocent?" I asked, biting my lip.

Her free hand reached down and rested on my bare thigh. "Honey, I've been in this business long enough. I know them when I see them."

"How many other girls are there?"

"There's enough, but we always want more. Especially ones like you." She stood. "Think about it, Andi. You have my card."

"Wait! I want to meet the others so I can think about it more." I didn't have time to think about it. This was it. I needed to get in with Jasmine, meet more girls, find out who Martinez was. There was a reason Leah and Nina had told me to stay away, and if my hunch was right, it was the reason I came to Vegas.

"I knew you'd be perfect. Meet us at PT's on E. Tropicana, Wednesday night at ten." With that, she left.

I stood and handed the valet attendant my claim ticket. I needed this lead to work or I'd be back to square one.

Chapter Fourteen

Paul

The entire time I was on my date, I was thinking about Andi on her date. It wasn't because I couldn't trust her. It was because I was thinking about her blowing…

Blowing *me* to be more specific.

We'd been seeing each other for a week and all we'd done was kiss. There was nothing wrong with that, but let's be real …

I wanted to fuck her.

I wanted to fuck her so fucking hard.

I wanted to be buried so deep inside her that she was screaming my name and the neighbors were questioning if they should call for help.

It had been weeks—hell, I think it was going on months since I'd last gotten laid, and I was aching. My hand wasn't doing the job anymore, and the more Andi strutted around in her short dresses and braless morning T-shirts, the more I was starting to lose it. I was trying not to show it when I was with her, but when I was alone in my bed at night, I worked myself *good.* I wanted Andi to work me, though. I wanted her hand, her mouth, her pussy—I wanted her to pleasure me, not my hand.

Andi wasn't home from her date when I got home from mine, so I went to shower. When I came out, she was in her shower and I was half-tempted to join her but decided against it. Instead, I went to the living room and waited for her to finish. When she came out—braless—my eyes drifted to her chest then to her eyes.

"Gorgeous," I greeted her.

"Sugar lips." She laughed.

I motioned for her to come cuddle with me on the couch and she did, but not before kissing me.

"Did you win?"

"Well, not me, but my client did."

"That's what I meant." I wrapped her in my arms so she was lying in front of me as I spooned her from behind.

"Can we talk about it in the morning? I'm exhausted." She sighed as she got comfortable against me.

I kissed her bare shoulder that was exposed from her tank top. "Yeah, gorgeous, we can."

"Can we also do something different tonight?"

My ears perked up, and so did my dick. "What's that?"

"Dating other people does suck and I was wondering if you'd sleep in my bed tonight?"

"You want me to sleep in your bed?" My smile widened.

"Well, it's bigger than this couch." She laughed.

"My bed is bigger than your bed." I teased.

"Then can we sleep in your bed?"

Was she really only referring to sleeping or was sleeping code for sex? Either way I wanted her in my bed.

"Yeah, baby, let's go to bed."

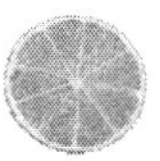

I woke with Andi asleep on my chest. When she said she wanted to sleep in my bed, she really did mean sleep. We crawled into my bed and the moment her head rested on my chest, she was out and I mean out. She snores a little and it's cute. I'd lightly run my fingertips along her arm, savoring Andi's body on mine until sleep overtook and I drifted off.

I had to piss when I woke, but I'd be damned if I was going to ruin this moment. Instead, I lightly ran my fingertips over her bare arm. She stirred and peeked up at me.

"Morning." I smiled.

"Are you always this happy in the morning?"

"Yes, especially with my girl on me."

"I see your cockiness is in full effect too."

"Oh, my cock is *definitely* in full effect." She groaned and started to roll off of me. "Where do you think you're going?"

"I need coffee to deal with all of this." She waved her hand up and down my body and I grabbed her wrist, tugging on her until she straddled my hips.

"You're not going anywhere until you at least kiss me."

"With morning breath?" she mumbled into my chest.

"I don't give a shit, woman."

I grabbed her cheeks and planted a firm kiss on her lips until she opened up and allowed my tongue to enter her mouth. If kissing her was all I was allowed to do for whatever reason, then I was going to love her mouth as if it was her fucking pussy. I sucked on her tongue, drawing it into my mouth as far as it would go until a moan escaped her. My hips pressed up, my dick hard and searching for that one spot it wanted to be. When I pressed it between her legs, she jumped, breaking our contact.

"Coffee," she mumbled and hurried out the door, leaving me hard and aching.

We both worked in the sex industry and I understood that not all chicks went around sleeping with guys, but I thought I'd made it clear that we were in a serious relationship. I wasn't sleeping with anyone else and I wanted to be with only her. I needed to make it clear that even though it had only been a week, a week was long enough for me.

We needed to get on the same page.

The week went on. Each night we slept together and by slept, I meant *slept.* So I came up with a plan.

"Honey, I'm home," I sang, coming in from the garage.

"I'm in the kitchen," she called back.

"We're so domesticated." I laughed. "What smells good?" I sniffed the air.

"I'm no *Food Network* chef so you're only getting tacos."

"That's perfect because I picked up this." I held up the bottle of Patrón.

"Want to get me drunk tonight?" She laughed.

I walked up behind her, brushed her hair to the side, and kissed her neck. "I heard tequila makes clothes fall off?"

"That's a song silly."

"Well, we're gonna find out."

I made us tequila with Coke, a squeeze of lime, and a dash of salt to go with our tacos. We were two drinks in, and I was four tacos deep when Andi asked the question I'd been avoiding since our first date.

"How long were you with her?"

I stared at her for a few seconds, not sure if I wanted to go down this road. I rubbed my hand down my face. "I guess it was almost two years. Maybe less."

"Was it recent?"

I gave a sarcastic laugh. "Nah, far from it. It was a long ass time ago."

"And you're still hung up on her?"

I drew in my eyebrows. "What gives you that idea?"

She took a sip of her drink. "Well, you haven't had a serious relationship since her."

"I haven't *wanted* one since her. Not until you, gorgeous."

She smiled and a blush crept up her neck. After a few moments and another sip of her drink she said, "If you went that long then she must have fucked you up good."

I smiled. "You really do ask a lot of questions."

"I'm only curious about the man I'm dating."

I chuckled. "You mean my past."

"More about how *he* became an escort."

And there we had it. The real meaning behind the question. "In high school—"

"High school?"

"I know, it was a long ass time ago. Just let me finish."

"Okay, go on." She stood and started to pour us both more drinks.

"I had a full ride for football to UCLA. I was going to turn pro, live happily ever after with her. You know, the American dream."

"What happened?"

She slid me my drink and I took a sip. I sighed before continuing. "We were in love, at least I thought we were. I'm not so sure she loved me. Before the end of football season, she got pregnant—"

"Oh, wow," she gasped.

I nodded. "Yeah, but you want to know what the bitch did?"

"What?" she whispered, a few of her fingers covering her mouth as if she already knew the answer.

I leaned back, closed my eyes and took a deep breath, calming myself so I could utter the words that continued to haunt me.

"It's okay. You don't need to tell me," she said and grabbed my hands in hers.

"It happened a long time ago. It still hurts to think about it."

She nodded.

"So yeah. She had an abortion which caused us to break up." I stared at our woven hands for a few beats and then took a few gulps of my drink until it was almost empty.

"Let's go to the living room." She held up the Patrón bottle.

I grinned at her then stood. "Body shots on the couch?"

"You and your body shots." She laughed then squealed the moment my hand smacked her ass.

"You and your body." I picked her up, carried her to the couch, then placed her so she was straddling my lap, still holding the tequila bottle.

"You like my body." She kissed me lightly.

"No, baby, I love your body." I returned my mouth to hers, my hands working their way up her jean clad legs and then under the hem of her T-shirt. The moment my hands skimmed her bare skin, she pulled her mouth from mine.

"Don't you want to know why I'm an escort, too?" she blurted.

"If you want to tell me."

She took a big swig of the tequila. "My mother was a whore and she got me into the game."

I stared at her. I wasn't sure if she was serious, but she wasn't smiling. "You're serious?"

She nodded. "Yeah, and this is why I don't sleep with my clients. I'm not a whore like she is."

Was this also why she hadn't slept with me? It was on the tip of my tongue to ask her, but the way she'd chugged the tequila indicated that maybe sex to her was something she waited to do. If she only knew how many clients and chicks I'd slept with…

I *was* a whore.

"You know you mean a lot to me, right?"

"I know, love bug."

I smiled. "Love bug?"

"Sugar lips?"

"Love bug is better." I chuckled and kissed her lips.

"Is it time to watch a movie now?"

"We can do whatever you want, gorgeous."

"I'm going to go put on my pajamas first."

While she changed, I put on basketball shorts, then turned on the TV as I waited for her. When she came out, she was dressed in short pajama shorts and a spaghetti strap top—braless. I groaned the moment I saw her because she was going to be the death of me.

Braless titties.

Bare legs.

Hard dick.

I needed my cock to calm down but, of course, all I could think about was the way she smelled of coconuts. Finally, she picked a movie and cuddled against my side. I pulled her so we were spooning because my dick needed to be against her ass. I wanted her back to my front so I had easy access to play with her.

I couldn't take the agony any longer. My hand slipped down the front of her body, searching. I eased up the front of her shirt to slip my hand in her shorts and she stopped me.

"It's okay," I whispered in her ear. "I'm gonna make you feel good, gorgeous." She turned slightly, her eyes searched mine almost as though she was unsure. "Just relax."

She stared at me for a beat and then smiled before she wiggled her hips against me. I nudge my dick against her firmly, causing her to moan and me to grind a little harder. "I fucking love hearing those noises from your mouth. I wanna hear more. Tell me I can make you come, gorgeous. I wanna hear my name leave your lips. I've been dying to taste you."

My hand slipped farther into her shorts and she turned onto her back, lifting her ass and allowing me to pull them off. Her gaze met mine as I lifted her shirt off before moving my mouth to hers, my hand cupping and kneading her breast. She moaned again, my tongue slipping in at that moment, and our kiss deepened. Her body relaxed and after a few moments I worked my way down her body with my mouth.

I dragged my tongue from her lips down her neck to her tits where I kneaded one perfect globe in one hand and sucked the other erect nipple. Her back arched and another moan came from her mouth.

When I switched to the other nipple, I noticed the ink across her rib cage:

she always had a way

with her brokenness

she would take her pieces

and make them beautiful

I made a mental note to ask her about it later because I didn't want to stop my path to her sweet spot. I trailed kisses and licked down her chest to her stomach, her hands finally fisted in my hair and I kissed lightly up her thigh, working my way to her pussy. Just as my hands touched her so I could spread her open and get my first taste, she slid up the couch and out of my grasp.

"I … I can't do this. I'm sorry," she quavered and took off out of the living room.

"Wait," I called after her. "What do you mean?" I followed.

"I'm sorry. I thought I could, but I can't." She closed her bedroom door.

"Baby, what's going on? Talk to me."

"I'm sorry," she apologized again. "It's not going to work out."

The hell it's not!

I tried the handle of her door, but it was locked. I didn't give a shit. She couldn't say this bullshit and then lock herself in her room. I'd confessed to her about Vanessa. The least she could do was tell me what it was about *me* that she found so repulsive. Without giving it another thought, I rammed my shoulder into the door and it popped opened. The lousy lock was no match for my size or my strength. She flinched as she stood next to the bed when I barged in.

"You don't get to do this," I declared.

"It's not about you!" she hissed, tears streaking down her face. She was holding a piece of paper that was recently folded into fours.

"The hell it's not!" I started to walk closer to her and she backed up, causing me to stop. "Are you scared of me?" She shook her head. "Then what is it? Why are you crying?"

She stared up at the ceiling for a beat then back to me. "If I told you my flaws would you still want to be with me?"

"Of course," I admitted without needing to think about it.

"They're really bad, Paul."

"So we're back to Paul now?"

She set the paper down on the bed and I saw that it was a drawing of a birthday cake—something a kid would have drawn and colored. She then crossed her arms over her chest and that's when I realized she was dressed in her normal tank top she wore to bed—not the spaghetti strap thing she had on earlier.

"What I'm about to tell you, you can't change. So don't even think you can. It's in the past. It's done. Just like your past, I can't change what happened with your high school girlfriend." I nodded. "These things make us who we are today and yes, I'm dealing with shit and before you… Just… I'm okay if you don't want to be with me anymore once you find out."

"Why do you keep saying that?"

"Because my mom sold my virginity when I was seventeen and I haven't had sex since!"

She fell to the floor, sobs coming from her throat. I rushed to her, scooping her up and carrying her to my room. "Shh, it's okay," I whispered, placing her in the center of my bed and wrapping her in my arms.

She cried until she fell asleep. I, on the other hand, didn't get a wink of sleep. All I could think about was how, even though this woman next to me was broken, I didn't care because I was certain I was falling in love with her.

Chapter Fifteen

Andi

The sun seeped through the blinds and my eyes felt dry and crusty as I tried to open them. My mouth was dry, my head pounded, and when I felt the warm, hard body pressed firmly against me, everything came crashing back.

I'd told Paul how I lost my virginity.

Well, I hadn't told him everything. I'd spared him the graphic details. I couldn't believe that I'd told him. I'd never told *anyone* about that night—not Cat, not even Seth. It might have been because of the tequila. It might have been because of Paul. It might have been the mixture of the two. I wasn't sure.

The feelings I felt were foreign to me. I wanted to tell him everything. I wanted to tell him about my mother, about Tony, and about Marco. I wanted to tell him about the FBI and how I was in Vegas undercover. How I was really Joselyn Marquez and not Andi Middlebrooke. But I couldn't tell him most of it, so I told him the only part I could tell him, and that was the only thing that no one knew.

"Hey," he said, tucking a piece of hair behind my ear. "Sleep okay?"

I shrugged. Sure I slept, but I didn't feel rested. "I guess."

"Do you want me to get you anything? Water? Coffee?"

"Water."

He left and I debated if I was going to tell him more about that God awful night. I wanted to. I felt that if I told him it would be a weight lifted off my shoulders. For so long I'd carried it around, hiding the secret from everyone. It was my secret, my past, my mask, but I was tired of wearing it, especially around the man I loved.

Loved…

That was the feeling I felt when I was with Paul. I'd never been in love before. I'd thought I loved Seth, but it was puppy love. He was my best friend. The feelings I had for Paul were completely and utterly different. This man was everything to me, and the moment he found out I was undercover, I was sure he wouldn't want anything to do with me.

I was lying to him nonetheless.

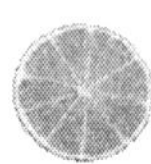

A few nights after my freak out, Autumn called Paul to invite us over for dinner. Internally, I was freaking out *again.* I didn't know why I was so nervous. If they were anything similar to what Paul described, I had a feeling I was going to fall just as hard and fast for them as I had for Paul. Besides, I'd went into this undercover operation after doing extensive research on everyone involved with S&R. I knew Gabe was once an escort but left after meeting Autumn, and the three of them were now running a self-defense company. So they had to be good people…

Right?

Paul and I didn't discuss the bomb I dropped on him. He was probably waiting for me to tell him on my own terms the rest of the story, which I *loved* about him. He had a way of making me *feel* loved and cherished. Even though he was hot for me because let's face it, he admitted it on several different occasions. He not only told me he cared for me, but that night when I had my freak out, he picked me up and carried me to bed, held me until I fell asleep and probably until long after, and *showed* me how much he actually cared for me. He could tell me all day how much he liked me, but I felt it and that meant more to me.

About ten minutes into the drive to Gabe and Autumn's house, Paul reached over and grabbed my fidgeting hands before my knuckles started bleeding. "Stop worrying so much, gorgeous. Gabe and Autumn are gonna love you."

"I'm sorry. It's just… I know that they mean a lot to you, and you mean a lot to me, so I'm only hoping I don't make an ass out of myself."

"Are you kidding? They're so damn excited I've got someone to bring for dinner, it's going to be impossible to make a bad impression. Knowing how I feel about you, I'm willing to bet they love you already."

Before I realized it, we were pulling into what I assumed was Gabe and Autumn's driveway. Paul put the *Jeep* in park and turned off the ignition. Just as I reached for the door handle, he grabbed my wrist and pulled me back. Keeping one hand on the steering wheel, he released my wrist from the other, grabbed the back of my neck and pulled me in to kiss me long and deep. Once my body started to relax, he backed away and gave me a panty dropping smile.

"Relax. Let's go have fun." I caught my breath and got out of the car, Paul came around the back and grabbed my hand. Once we made it to the door, Paul walked in without knocking. I looked at him and he laughed. "What? He's like my brother."

I laughed. "I didn't say anything."

We walked into the kitchen and the boys greeted each other by sharing a bro-hug before Paul made his way to Autumn, "Auttie!" He gave her a tight but brief hug and a peck on her cheek, then he grabbed my hand and pulled me to his side, wrapping an arm around my lower back. "Guys, this is my girl, Andi. Andi, this is Gabe and his beautiful fiancé, Autumn."

Autumn came to me and wrapped me in a hug so tight it was hard for me to breath for a moment. "It's great to finally meet you, Andi. Let's make some margaritas before dinner's ready." She linked arms with me and led the way to the bar.

Being around Gabe and Autumn was effortless. Paul, Gabe, and Autumn had a friendly banter that I loved to watch. Sometimes I would join in when I felt comfortable enough to get involved. They told me about their business and offered to teach me a few self-defense moves to stay protected while out with clients. I wanted to tell them it wasn't necessary, that I probably had more training than them, but instead I thanked them and Paul being Paul said he would show me some—naked.

After dinner, we all sat around the table sipping on our drinks. Paul had his usual tequila and coke, Gabe was sipping on what I thought was a whiskey and coke, and Autumn had made us two different batches of margaritas: one with alcohol, the other without.

As we sat around the dining room table, the boys shootin' the shit, Paul looked at Autumn with a smile on his face. "So have you guys been to the doctor yet? I'm dying to know when my niece or nephew will be making an appearance."

Well, that explains the virgin margaritas…

"We just went last week. Our little monkey will arrive in about seven months."

When I took a quick glance at Paul, I saw *it*. I couldn't decide if it was envy or pain because just as fast as I saw it, it was gone.

Autumn brought both of her hands down on the table and stood, "Why don't you guys make your way to the living room while I clean up." As she started making her way to the kitchen, Gabe wrapped an arm around her hips and dragged her down to his lap.

"Angel, leave it. I'll get it. You need to take it easy. That's my unborn child you're carrying."

"I'm not gonna break. Promise."

She wrapped her hands around his neck and plastered a kiss to his lips that made me blush. These two were an obvious power couple. The love displayed made me envious, but watching the love exchanged between the two of them caused me to worry. It reminded me that I was in love with Paul, but I hadn't told him *everything*.

Wanting out of my own head, I stood and offered to help. As I walked past Paul to gather a few dishes, he slid his hand from my back to my hip and gave it a little squeeze. He pulled me down and whispered in my ear, "I'm glad you're here with me tonight, gorgeous." He kissed my cheek, letting his lips linger for a moment, so I turned and pressed my lips to his, then smiled and made my way to the kitchen.

When I walked in, Autumn was already washing the dishes she had brought in. She looked at me and smiled. "I've never seen Paul with a girlfriend before." She laughed.

Her confession brought a smile to my face. "I don't think he had a choice. I kinda barged in on him."

She turned the water off, grabbing a dish towel to dry her hands "Paul's… How do I put this lightly?" She thought for a moment, looking past me. "Like I said, I've never seen him with a girlfriend before. Just don't hurt him, okay?"

I couldn't do anything but stare at the floor. I couldn't defend myself because in the end, when everything came out, I had no doubt he would be hurt.

And *that* would destroy me.

"He doesn't think we see it. I mean, we know he was burned badly in the past, but I have a feeling it was worse than the details he gave us." She walked up and placed her hand on my arm to get my attention. "I'll save you the details, but if there's one thing I've learned in my experience, it's how to recognize someone who has been through so much it almost broke them."

The conversation started about Paul, but the way she was looking at me made me wonder if she knew about *me* and what I'd been through—maybe it was about her. "Everybody needs somebody, Andi." She continued. "Sometimes it takes the right person to make you realize it." She looked toward the living room where the guys were laughing and smiled. Shaking her head, she grabbed the two pitchers of margaritas. "Come on, let's go see what the boys are up to."

I told Paul I was meeting the girls. It was only a half-lie. I was meeting the girls, but he assumed it was Leah and Nina when really it was Martinez's crew. I still had a job to do, I just hoped I didn't get my heart broken in the process. If I was right and Martinez was the man in charge of the operation, then Paul would soon find out who I really was and everything would change. But he'd expressed numerous times that he no longer wanted to be an escort, so we *could* make us work. I knew we could.

When I arrived at PT's, I scanned the restaurant for Jasmine. She was sitting at a moon shaped booth, sipping a cocktail. She waved me over and I slid in. I expected her to be sitting with a few girls because I wanted to meet with more than just her, but she was alone.

She reached over to give me a hug in greeting and I hugged her back. "Honey, it's good to see you again."

"Where are the others?" I asked.

"Oh, they're coming. You know how chicks are. Always need to make sure they look good before leaving the house." She laughed and took a sip of her drink.

Was I off base here? Were these girls just regular hookers out to make a buck? I wasn't quite sure what I was looking for in the sense of trafficking. Jasmine had said I would make three times what I was making at S&R, but what did that really entail?

"I seemed to make it on time." I laughed.

"You've yet to reach this level. Let's get you a drink and talk." She flagged down the waitress and I ordered a margarita. "Now let's get one thing straight." She took a sip of her vodka and water. "If you choose to go on a date we set up, there's no turning back. You work for Martinez, you do your job, and there are no problems. He'll take care of you. Fuck up once? You better hope he can't find you."

As Jasmine was talking, I envisioned Martinez as your typical pimp. The kind who would slap you around when you didn't pay or when you didn't do your *job* correctly. I thought that maybe this would be my *in;* a way for me to find out more about the trafficking situation. As if right on cue, the group of girls we were meeting walked in and I overheard part of a conversation that peaked my interest.

"… Nelly is gone. That fucker sold her! We made the money we needed too and he still fucking sold her!"

Before I knew what was happening, Jasmine slide from the booth, pulled the girls aside and whispered something that looked like the fear of God in them. I didn't know what was said, but after what just went down, I was certain Martinez was the guy I was after.

"What was that about?" I asked Jasmine as she slid back into the booth.

"Remember what I said about fucking up?" I nodded. "Her friend fucked up." She glared at the girl who had talked about Nelly.

This was definitely the crew I needed to get involved with to learn about the trafficking that was going on.

The question was: How deep was I willing to go?

Chapter Sixteen

Paul

When I checked my back office for the week, I nearly had a stroke. A regular from Malibu had booked for Thursday night because she was going to be in town for a bachelorette party and wanted me to meet up with her.

Regular meant sex.

Any other time this would be okay, but now that I was dating Andi, this was horrible. But I couldn't cancel because I had a long term relationship with this chick, and I at least owed it to her to show up and bring a guy with me for her to fuck. It would be a win-win for her. She would see me and she would still get laid, but she'd only pay for one of us.

I called up my buddy Nick and told him the game plan for Thursday.

"I'll try to be home early." I kissed Andi's lips, savoring the feel. I didn't want to leave her at home. I wanted to stay with her and watch movies—make her feel safe, comfortable. Ever since she'd told me about how her mom she sold her virginity, it was always in the back of my mind. I only wanted to protect her even if it was seventeen years ago. I just had that instinct now.

"You have a job to do, love bug, and I have a date on Saturday. Nothing changes."

"We don't need to do this job anymore, baby. I have my job with Gabe and Autumn. You can work with us, too."

She laughed. "What do you think I can do?"

I shrugged. "I don't know. Book new clients for us?"

She pushed on my chest. "Go have fun."

I stopped walking, remembering I hadn't told her who my date was with. I never needed to tell her before, but this one felt as though I should. I turned back to her. "Gorgeous …"

She looked at me from the TV, "Yeah?"

"I think I should tell you who my date's with."

Her eyebrows scrunched in confusion. "Okay?" I walked over to her, sat on the coffee table in front of her and grabbed her hands. "You're scaring me," she whispered, looking into my eyes.

Reaching up, I brushed a piece of her brown hair behind her ear. "It's not like that. She's a client from Malibu."

She stared at me, realization dawning across her face. "Oh," she whispered.

"I'm not like that anymore."

"I know."

"I called Nick. He's going with me and he's gonna take care of business."

Her gaze darted to mine. "You called Nick?"

"I'm not going to sleep with her if that's what you're thinking."

"But—"

"Just because we're not having sex doesn't mean I need to fuck clients. I lov … I love being with you and I want to see where this goes. I'm not going to fuck it up only to have sex. My hand is doing a good job." I smiled at her hoping she'd laugh.

She looked up from wringing her hands that were in her lap. "It's not that I don't *want* to have sex. I'm scared."

I tilted her face, grabbing her chin lightly so she had to look me in the eyes. "I know, and we'll take this slow. We have forever."

"Right, *forever*." She sighed.

"Forever, gorgeous." I kissed her one last time and then I left to meet Nick at the Bellagio where we were meeting Brina, my client at The Bank where she wanted to be picked-up at a nightclub as though she didn't know who I was. Part of it were true; she didn't know Nick.

We waited in line to enter the club. It sucked being a guy in Vegas. The women got special treatment while men got the short end of the stick, especially if we weren't with a group of females.

"Don't you have connections here?" I asked Nick.

"Yeah, but I don't see him."

I groaned. This wasn't how I wanted to start off the night. I wanted to get in and get out. Nick this is Brina. You two fuck, have a nice night, peace out.

"Let me text him," he remarked, pulling out his phone.

I checked mine. I didn't have a set time to be inside the club. Brina knew I'd show. The plan was to surprise her, dance with her, seduce her, fuck her in the bathroom or something and then leave. I was going to do the surprise and dancing parts while Nick did the dancing, seducing and fucking parts. The plan was foolproof.

"All right, he's coming out."

A guy came out the doors a few minutes later and waved us over. We went to the front of the line as people groaned. The bouncer unhooked the red velvet rope and after Nick had introduced me to his buddy, we entered a hallway and into an elevator. The bass of the music thumped as the elevator rose to the nightclub.

"What does she look like again?" Nick asked as the elevator lifted floor by floor.

I shrugged. "You know, a blonde babe from Cali with big boobs."

"My type." He laughed.

"The trick is to find her." I chuckled because really finding anyone in a dark nightclub in Vegas was like finding a needle in a haystack.

"Let's get a drink first."

The doors opened. "Fuck yeah."

The space was packed as we entered the two-story club. People stood around the upper deck, mingling, dancing and waiting to order at the upstairs bar. We made our way as I scanned each face looking for Brina, but I didn't see her. I hoped I didn't see her because if I did then the situation would be awkward and would throw off the plan.

After waiting ten excruciating minutes and scanning the dark club for Brina, we finally squeezed in between two chicks to order our drinks.

"Hi," one purred.

"Sugar." I nodded.

"Whatcha drinkin'?" She eyed my tequila and coke.

"A charro negro." She looked at me as if I'd lost my mind. "I've never heard of that. Can I try it?"

Did she just ask to try my drink? "You're asking for trouble, sugar."

"What happens in Vegas stays in Vegas, right?"

I caught the eye of Nick over this chick's shoulder and took a deep breath. "Not with me." I nudged my head for Nick to follow and we walked toward the railing where the upstairs looked down onto the dance floor. I was off my game and all thoughts were on Andi. I didn't want to do the escort shit anymore, even if Andi and I didn't work out. This wasn't my scene anymore. As I scanned the bodies gyrating to the music, the lights changing colors and the disco ball reflecting from above, I spotted Brina and a few girls sitting in a booth next to the dance floor.

"See the blonde in the black dress with her hair pulled in a high ponytail?" I shouted over the music, pointing toward where Brina was sitting in the booth. "She just took a shot of whatever that is on the table."

"Yeah, man. You sure you want to give her up to me? I mean. I'm all for hittin' that." He took a sip of his drink.

"I'm going to get out of the game."

"Aw fuck. You too?" He shook his head in disapproval. "First Gabe and now you?"

I laughed. "Chicks, man."

He chuckled. "I'm never falling in love."

"Never say never. I didn't think I would be in love again."

"Enough of this love talk. Let's do this shit so I can get laid."

"All right. Pound your drink. We're gonna get dirty on the dance floor."

"Never say that to me again." He chugged his drink.

We walked down the stairs then weaved in and out of bodies on the dance floor as we made our way to the table where Brina was. The club was packed. People were all around dancing, kissing—some maybe more. My plan was to tell Brina that I'd noticed her from across the room and ask her to dance, but as I got closer, she stood and joined her friends on the dance floor. I came up behind her and whispered in her ear, "Sugar," Nick came around to the front of us, caging her in, "this is my friend, Nick."

Our bodies began to sway to the beat of the music, her head rested on my shoulder, her gaze locked with Nick's. Normally my hands would be roaming her body, getting her worked up, but I needed Nick to take this one. I wasn't into it. I caught his eye and motioned for him to do just that. His hands worked up and down her sides, our bodies still gyrating to the music and then my body went rigid.

What the fucking fuck?

It took me a second to register what, better yet *who* I was looking at. There *she* was dressed in white—a color I'd always thought I'd see her walk down the aisle in on the day *we* said "I do." A sash was across her body that read "Bride to Be". My gaze darted to hers and everything clicked into place as she stood next to the table that Brina had just left. They were here for *her* bachelorette party before Vanessa got married—married to someone else.

Vanessa gave me a tight smile and waved. I stood still as Brina rubbed her ass on my crotch. I didn't know if I *could* smile or wave back at Vanessa. "Hey!" Nick slapped me on the back of the head. "Are you going to dance or what?"

"I gotta go."

I started to walk away and Vanessa grabbed my wrist. "PJ, wait!"

I stared down into her dark eyes. "I gotta go."

"You're still mad after all this time?"

I reached up and ran my fingers along the hem of the sash. "I don't know what I am, Ness."

"Can we talk, please?"

I stared at her, not saying anything. When she left my house our senior year, we'd never spoken again. We'd never had closure. Now she was staring me in the eyes, wanting to talk, and for what? I'd thought about this moment so many times, wondered what I'd say, what I'd do. But now that the moment had arrived, I realized I had nothing to say. None of it mattered anymore. I just wanted to go home and be with Andi.

"PJ..."

"Nothing to talk about, Ness." I knew what I wanted. What I needed—*who* I needed. And she wasn't anywhere in this nightclub. "I gotta go. My girl's waiting for me." I smiled a genuine smile. "I really am happy for you, Vanessa. Congratulations."

I turned toward Nick to give him a head nod, letting him know I was out. I was going home. Fuck the closure. She'd killed us and whatever future we may have had when she'd had the abortion. End of story. We didn't need to talk. I'd moved on—finally. I didn't need women, tequila or a pocket full of cash anymore.

I only needed Andi.

I was on autopilot as I pulled into the garage and killed the engine. I didn't have a plan. My heart was pounding. My throat was tightening. My eyes were stinging, and if Andi walked out because she got the wrong idea, I was going to lose my fucking mind.

I took a deep breath, got out of the *Jeep* and walked into the house. Andi was laying on the couch watching TV. "Hey. You *are* home early."

I didn't say anything. I still wasn't sure what I was going to say. I felt as though I was hiding the situation from her, but I just couldn't come out and tell her. I reached my hand out to her.

"What's wrong?"

"Come with me."

She looked down at my hand and then took it. "Are you okay?"

"Just … I need you."

"Okay."

She took my hand and I led her to my room and then the en-suite bathroom. I smelled of smoke, sweat, and I wanted her naked.

"Paul…" she uttered.

"Please," I begged, turning her so her back was against the wood bathroom door. She looked up at me, her beautiful amber colored eyes staring back, questioning me. "We can go slow. No sex. I just want to feel your body against mine."

She finally nodded and I stripped her of her shirt, followed by mine, then took her mouth. She whimpered, her back pressed against the door, my body aching to be inside her. When I lifted my head, I realized she *was* wearing a bra.

"Rhinestones?" I smiled.

She bit her lower lip. "Do you like it?"

"You wore this for me?"

"I thought about what you said. About how you used to sleep with clients and since this one was a regular and you—" I silenced her with my mouth. "I'm not sure about sex, though," she mumbled against my lips.

"That's okay, gorgeous. We're gonna go as far as we can." She nodded and I grabbed the elastic of shorts, looking her in her eyes. "Ready?"

"Yes," she breathed.

I pulled her shorts down, revealing black lace panties that matched her black lace bra, minus the rhinestones. It was a sight that I would forever have burned in my memory. "Fuck, baby. You're beautiful."

She blushed and I kissed her again, this time softer, emphasizing how much I loved her and not just how much I wanted her body. I pulled back, looking into her eyes again. This was the time. This was the time for me to tell her. I had to tell her before sex—or whatever this led to.

"Andi," I beamed, my hands on her cheeks.

"Yeah?"

"From the moment your smart mouth barged into my house, I fell in love with you. I had no idea that my new roommate would be the woman I wanted to spend every second of every day with, but she was. We both have had a shitty past, but I don't care. I want you in my future. I love you. I love you so fucking much."

A tear trickled down her cheek and I reached up, wiping it away. "I love you—"

I didn't let her finish her speech. I didn't need it. I just needed the three words. My hands wrapped behind her back, unclasping her bra, then I pulled her into the shower, turning it on as our mouths stayed locked. Freezing water shot out of the shower head, but I barely noticed as my tongue danced with hers. My body was on fire. My hands kneaded her breasts, my fingers pinched her nipples and she moaned, her head tilting back as she broke our kiss.

I adjusted the water and once I got it perfect I realized I still had my jeans and shoes on plus Andi had her panties on. Making quick work, I removed our soaked clothes, tossing them onto the bathroom floor. My dick stood at attention ready to play, my balls ached and my mouth watered—I wanted to devour her in every way possible.

My gaze flicked up to meet hers, but she was looking down at my cock. "Give me your hand." Her head snapped to look at me. "It's okay."

Timidly she reached out and I took it, bringing it to my mouth and placed a kiss on her palm then ran it down my chest, the water from the shower letting it slide easily over each ripple of my abs. Her gaze never left her palm as she watched her hand go lower and lower. Just before we reached my shaft, I looked up to find Andi's eyes already looking into mine. I could see the apprehension and nervousness she was feeling. After a brief nonverbal exchange, she lowered her gaze back down. I watched her reaction as her hand finally wrapped around the head of my dick. She sucked in a breath, bit her lip and then …

She licked her lips.

I smiled as I worked our hands back and forth over my cock. Once we started moving in one fluid motion, I removed my hand. Without my guidance, her soft hand glided effortlessly with the water and I groaned, my balls growing tight. I wasn't sure how long I would last with my girl working me.

"Fuck, gorgeous, that feels so good, don't stop."

I braced myself with my arm against the tiled wall, enjoying her strokes as she worked the tension from my body. I wanted to give her pleasure in return, but I didn't want to overwhelm her, so I focused on what she was okay with and that was loving her with my mouth. I kissed her, using my tongue until I couldn't hold out anymore and I came, jerking until I was spent and could barely stand.

Chapter Seventeen

Andi

I woke to a hand rubbing the inside of my thigh.

Drip.

Drip.

Drip.

After our shower the night before, we'd gone to sleep. I still didn't know what happened on his date to cause Paul to come home the way he did and I wasn't going to ask. When he was ready to tell him, he would—I'd hoped.

Being able to be the one he came home to, to be the one he *wanted*, to be the one he *needed*, felt empowering. He told me he loved me, I loved him and wanted to tell him everything.

Everything.

And I almost did, but he silenced me with his mouth and then we did naughty things and before I knew it, he was *drained* and we were sleeping.

We still hadn't had sex. However, I was ready. So ready. Especially after seeing his body last night in the shower and the way he gently took control but allowed me to also have control. It was nothing like twelve years ago.

I trusted him.

I trusted him completely.

"Andi," he whispered into my ear.

"Hmm?" I asked, trying to form a coherent thought.

"I need to tell you more about last night."

My back stiffened. He rolled onto his back, his hand leaving my thigh and I almost groaned out of protest.

Had he slept with his client then came home and told me he loved me?

"The part about my client went as planned." He paused for a long time and I wasn't sure if he was going to continue. I looked over at him and he was staring up at the ceiling, maybe lost in thought.

"My client was in town for a bachelorette party," he paused, sighed and then dropped the bomb, "for Vanessa."

I raised up on one elbow and faced him. "You saw Vanessa?"

He turned his head toward me. "Yeah. She wanted to talk, too."

"About what?"

He shrugged. "I don't know. I didn't talk to her other than telling her I didn't want to talk to her."

"You didn't?"

"Why would I?" He raised up on his elbow so we were face-to-face. "What is there to say? It's been almost fifteen years and I'm in love with you."

"What if she didn't get the abortion?"

He stared at me for a beat then laughed. "Oh, she did. She shoved her discharge papers in my face without a word after it happened when she returned to school."

"You're not curious what she wanted to talk to you about?"

"She didn't even know I was going to be there. It couldn't have been that important."

"True. But it fucked you up."

"I just wasn't expecting it." I nodded. "Let's never speak of her again."

I bit my lower lip and looked down at his bare chest. I was still turned on from his hand that was rubbing between my legs when I woke up and seeing his bare, rippled chest was an added bonus. Hooking my leg over his hip, I started to crawl over his body, causing him to lie back on his back.

"Andi." He grinned.

"Shh, I'm ready."

"You're ready, ready?"

I nodded then raised up, pulling my tank top over my head and tossing it to the floor. His hands rubbed along my bare back as my breasts slid across his chest, our mouths returning to savor each other. I wanted to stay locked together like glue, be with him in this position with me on top forever, his hands in my hair, mine in his, the sound of our lips smacking when we needed air.

My hips started to move, grinding on his cock. He groaned and deepened the kiss, his fingers dipped into the sides of my panties and he began to tug. I didn't hesitate as I moved back and forth. I was ready. This was it. This was the moment. I was tired of living in the past just as he was done living in his.

With our lips never losing contact, he rolled me over onto my back, his hips between my legs. He supported himself on one elbow as the other played with the elastic on my panties.

"Are you sure?"

Hoping it would get the message across, I grinned and lifted my hips, giving him permission to finish undressing me. He returned his mouth to mine and I felt a tug and the tickle of the lace from my underwear on the backside of my legs as he removed them, causing goosebumps to spread. Paul dropped them on the side of the bed then started at my ankles, running his fingertips along the outside of my leg until he reached my hip. A small moan escaped my lips, causing me to break the war our tongues were having.

He kept his forehead resting against mine. "Still the best fucking noise I've ever heard. I wanna hear more."

He brought a hand up and cupped one of my breasts, lowering his lips to the other. He started grinding his hips against my core at the same time he twisted the bud of my nipple.

I threw my head back and gasped. "Oh God."

"Shh. It's okay, baby. Just feel." Taking one of his hands, he started at my collarbone and traced random patterns down the front of me, circling around each nipple while he blew on them and caused them to pucker. "You're so fucking sexy," he mumbled as he started making his way back down to my chest with his mouth. His fingers started a path down to my stomach and the second his fingers came into contact with the swollen lips of my pussy, I jerked.

"Get out of your pretty little head, gorgeous, and just feel. I got you."

I nodded, my eyes closing as he slid down my body. He cupped my mound with his hand, letting me get a feel of him. Without saying a word, he ran two fingers back over my center, applying the smallest amount of pressure to the sweet spot my body was craving.

"That's it, baby," he cooed. "Just feel." He lowered his fingers again and after a second of teasing, he inserted a single digit. "So fucking wet. Christ, gorgeous…" Slowly pumping his finger in and out of me, he started peppering kisses along the inside of my thigh, slowly making his way toward my core. Once he got to where he wanted to be, he removed his finger and took one long swipe of his tongue.

"Paul…" I moaned.

He brought his hands up and used his thumb to spread me open for him. He started flicking my clit with his tongue before latching onto it with his mouth and alternating between flicking and sucking. His fingers probed my throbbing pussy again, starting with one and quickly adding another. The second he twisted his fingers into the perfect position, hitting just the right spot, my back arched off the bed and I screamed.

I grabbed his face, pulled him to me, and kissed him as if it were my last breath. Tasting myself on him only drove my need and hunger to have him inside of me. With our lips locked, he removed his boxers, and the feel of his hard cock grinding against where my body needed him most almost sent me directly into another frenzy. I wanted him bad. So fucking bad.

Paul pulled a condom out of his nightstand, ripping it open and rolling it on. Once he returned his lips to mine, he rolled us over again so I was on top. I knew why he did this, and damn if it didn't make me fall in love with him that much more.

He grabbed my face with both hands, staring me directly in the eyes, "I love you, Andi."

I wanted to tell him at that moment that my name was really Joselyn. Hear him say the words that I'd never heard before: "I love you, Joselyn." Instead, I asked a question I wasn't sure how to ask so I just did.

"Will you help me?"

A smile—the kind of smile I'd never seen on somebody's face before—smile of deep, consuming and devoted love, happiness and acceptance crossed his face. "I'm right here, baby."

I lifted just enough for him to reach around to ready himself, and then slowly I lowered myself onto him. I stared directly into his eyes as I lowered myself inch by inch, steadying myself with my hands on his chest. It burned as his dick stretched me, the size of him overtaking my pussy.

"That's it. Just go slow."

It was nothing like my first time. The pain might be comparable on some sort of level, but Paul was allowing me to get used to his size. It wasn't forced and out of my control. This was all me. I was staring into the eyes of the man I loved. The man I wanted to be with for the rest of my life.

The lower I got, the less the burn ached. Once I was filled to the hilt, emotions came flooding through me. Tears poured down my face and I tried with everything in me to keep them at bay, but it was no use. I was happy, relieved.

Paul sat up and wrapped me in his arms. He simply held me while I cried, rubbing circles on my back while my tears ran down his. We stayed like that for a few minutes, Paul inside of me until I was done crying. He looked me in the eyes and I nodded.

He began thrusting his hips, never once losing eye contact with me until I threw my head back when my orgasm tore through me. Paul followed moments later as he grabbed my hips, pumped hard a few times, and stilled.

I collapsed on top of him.

I was emotionally and physically exhausted, but so utterly and deeply in love.

Paul and I woke up the next morning in a tangled mess. If someone saw us, they wouldn't have been able to tell where I ended and Paul began. Throw the sheets in the mix and I wasn't sure if we'd ever be able to untangle. That was okay with me; I was right where I wanted to be.

Paul was laying on his back with half of my body thrown over his and my head on his chest. *This* was what it felt like to be in love. This man had my heart—my whole heart—and it scared the shit out of me. As fast and hard as I fell for him, I realized there was a chance that when he discovered everything (because eventually he would), I might lose him. The thought alone made my heart feel as if it was being ripped from my chest. Paul shifted slightly underneath me and abruptly brought me out of my thoughts.

When he moved, I felt the evidence of a hard-on rubbing against the leg I had thrown over his hips and I smiled at the memory of what had happened the night before. Every time I moved in the slightest, I felt the soreness between my legs. It wasn't like the first time. It hurt, but this time it was because of pleasure, not pain.

I lifted my hand from his chest and started tracing the lines of his abs. Wanting to see his face, I slowly lifted my head off his chest. I found him smiling and already looking down on me.

"Good morning, gorgeous."

"Good morning, sexy." I blushed.

"It's sexy now, is it?" He lifted me the rest of the way so I was completely on top of him, forcing my knees to fall on either side of his hips.

I shrugged. "I'm still trying to find what works, besides," I smiled and teased him by grinding my hips, "you *are* incredibly sexy, so it fits."

He wrapped his arms around me and flipped us so I was on my back underneath him. I started in a fit of laughter, loving our little power struggle, but when I looked up at him, he wasn't laughing. He gave me another one of those looks that caused butterflies the size of Texas to flutter around in my stomach and caused my heart to squeeze. He brought his hands up while keeping his elbows on the bed to support himself, and cleared the hair from my face.

"You're incredible, you know that?"

I leaned up and planted a hard kiss on his lips. When he started moving his hips, I threw my head back and let out something between a small moan and a gasp.

Paul brought his lips down to my ear and roughly whispered, "Are you still sore? Because I had all intentions of letting you rest this morning to give your pussy a break, but seeing you on top of me naked made me want to bury my dick so deep inside you and ride you so fucking hard you don't know your own fucking name."

I wrapped my arms around his neck and lifted my hips to rub against his now rock hard cock.

It was all the invitation he needed.

Looking in the mirror with my towel wrapped around me, I was doing the finishing touches to my makeup for my first date with one of Martinez's guys. Jasmine had given me some good tips on how the women in his crew should look. I had perfected the smoky look for my eye shadow, applying a thin line of eyeliner and mascara with just enough blush and a deep red color to my lips. By the time I was done, I barely recognized myself.

I walked out of the bathroom and to my closet. Jasmine had taken me out a few nights ago and walked me through a bunch of stores, trying to help me find the right look.

"This one!" She held up a small, skin-tight yellow dress with a halter top. "With your skin complexion, your makeup done right, and the right shoes, this would look amazing on you. I'll meet you at the register."

"Wait, I'm not going to be able to bend over in that thing without my goods

hanging out."

She gave me a creepy smile. "That's the whole point, honey."

I took a deep breath as I pulled the dress out of the closet and hung it on one of the knobs of my dresser. After putting it on and clasping the halter behind my neck, I put my heels on and stood to look in the mirror. *Damn!* I looked down to fix a part of the dress that I noticed was twisted and when I lifted my gaze back up to the mirror, Paul was walking by and he stopped short when he got to the entrance to my room wearing nothing but grey sweats riding low on his hips. I took in the sight of his chiseled abs as he stepped into the doorway and eyed me from head to toe.

"Damn, baby…"

Not wanting Paul to pick up on my worry, I sashayed my way over to him adding a little more sway into my hips than normal, and gave him a peck on the lips, "It's only a date, sexy. I promise I'll be home as soon as I can. And don't worry, I'll be thinking of you the entire time." I gave him a wink. "Love you," I sang before I turned to walk away.

He grabbed my wrist, twirled me back around and grabbed my face with both hands, kissing the ever loving daylight out of me. In typical Paul fashion, he kept our foreheads connected when he pulled back from the kiss. "I love you too, gorgeous. Please be careful."

"I will." I smiled at him and quickly turned to leave.

The moment I got in my car, I let out a deep, long sigh. I was scared shitless.

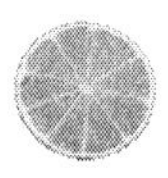

I pulled up to the Wynn hotel. I couldn't believe I was doing this again. This wasn't like my typical date with S&R. This was going into a hotel room knowing I would have to turn this client down for sex. I had to do this, though. My job depended on it. I'd decided to leave my gun at home. Even though this was a date with someone that was on Martinez payroll, I didn't want to be patted down and have them find my weapon and all hell break loose. Of course, I could say the gun was for protection, but this was my first date for them and I needed to build Jasmine's and Martinez's trust. I needed to get in good and find out what was going on, build my case and call in my team.

After my internal pep talk, I took a deep breath, squared my shoulders and waited for the valet to open the car door. Due to the detailed instructions I'd received in the fake email address I'd used for Jasmine, I knew exactly where I had to go to meet my john.

Go to the desk and give your name. There will be a key waiting for you. Pour yourself a drink when you get to the room. Don't be late.

I did as the email instructed and received a key for room 2316. Taking a deep breath, I pressed the button for the elevator and waited. My palms were clammy as I held my clutch purse and my feet were already aching in my sky-high heels. My seventeenth birthday flashed in my head, but I shook the memories off. I was older now—more experienced. This was different. This was by choice.

It was my *job*.

I walked in and pressed the button to the twenty-third floor. Giving myself one last once over, I made sure my yellow halter top dress was adjusted just right, my dark brown hair had enough volume and added one last coat of red lipstick.

The elevator door dinged, letting me know I had reached my floor. I followed the signs to the room number, doing my best not to trip over my own feet in the three and half inch stilettos I chose to wear. I slid the key in the door and let myself in. The wine was sitting in an ice bucket with a single glass next to it. I hadn't drunk any since the night of my birthday, not wanting to bring back the memory.

I walked further in, trying to shake off my nerves. The suite was larger than your typical hotel room—almost like a two bedroom apartment. I walked toward the living room to set my purse down on the table where the wine chilled, passing a private massage room, a half bath, and a kitchenette.

I wanted to get the date started, so I set my purse down a little harder than intended to give my john a heads up I was there and poured myself a small glass of the white wine. I was terrified, but I needed to keep a clear head to get through the night.

Marco's voice from seventeen years ago rang in my ears as I poured the wine. *"You want to hold it by the stem so the wine doesn't heat up by your body heat."*

When I lifted the wine glass to my lips, I saw someone come into the room out of the corner of my eye, then I felt him stop behind me before I could turn around. He grabbed my arms with a little more force than I expected and caused the glass to crash to the tiled floor.

He leaned down so his lips were against the shell of my ear, "Don't fucking move."

His voice was as cold as ice and I stopped breathing as fear instantly rose from the pit of my stomach. I could feel every finger of his hands digging into my skin and I knew it was going to leave bruises. This was not right; this was not what I signed up for and shit was about to go downhill—fast.

Still holding me from behind, he started walking us out of the room, the glass crunching beneath our shoes.

"What abou—"

He gave me a sharp yank back, causing me to slightly trip and land against him. It was like hitting a brick wall and instantly sent a pain down my spine.

"Quiet. I didn't give you permission to talk. You will only speak when I say you can. Now be a good little slut and do as you're told."

He threw me against the wall face first, my arms bracing the impact. Grinding his hips into my backside, giving me a glimpse of what the night was going to bring, he released me from his death grip and gave me a shove that sent me in the direction of the love seat faster than I anticipated, causing me to trip. I landed on my knees, catching the edge of the coffee table with my hand.

Fuck!

My body was sent into instant panic mode, I was terrified. This was not how the night was supposed to go down. I knew the shit Martinez's girls were into, but this went beyond my comfort zone. I was expecting to offer companionship for the night, and the possibility of him bringing up negotiations for sex but turning him down.

What the fuck was I going to do now? How in the hell was I going to get myself out of this?

I was finally able to find my footing and stood, facing the couch. I didn't dare turn to face him. My legs felt like Jell-O and I had to lean up against the plush seat cushion for support.

"Sit," he ordered.

Like a deer in the headlights of an eighteen wheeler, I couldn't move. My feet felt as if they were stuck in cement pillars.

"Did you hear what I just said, bitch? Sit!" The boom in his voice when he gave the last command was like a gunshot going off in my head and I did the first thing that I could think of—I ran.

When I got to the door, I twisted the handle and yanked. It had budged only a crack before a large hand slammed it shut. The other hand twisted into the back of my hair and jerked me back.

"You stupid slut! Lucky for you, I like it when they fight." He wrapped his free arm around my middle and started dragging me down a hall to what I assumed was the bedroom.

I kicked. I screamed. I tried to break free. It was no use.

He threw me onto the bed, straddled my hips and grabbed both of my arms and held them above my head. That was the first time I saw what he looked like as I continued to scream, twisting and turning, trying with everything in me to wiggle out from under him. He looked nothing like what I'd thought he would. He had the most piercing blue eyes I'd ever seen, perfect teeth when he would give me his evil smile, and even though we'd fought a little, his hair was still perfect on his head. This man could have been any woman's boyfriend. Instead, he was committing a crime.

Still holding both of my wrists with one hand, he brought the other down and squeezed my cheeks. "Scream all you want, slut. It's only gonna fucking turn me on that much more."

He turned my head to the side and licked me from my collarbone to my earlobe. Bile rose up my throat and the tears started flowing. A sob broke free when he started to pump his hips. Removing his hand from my face, he grabbed the front of my yellow dress and yanked, causing the clasps from around my neck to break and giving him access to my breasts.

"Fuck, yeah. Just like I imagined. Fucking gorgeous." He pulled my strapless bra down as well.

Gorgeous.

Paul.

What the fuck was I doing?

I was a trained FBI agent. I had a man who loved me, who made love to me. I wasn't going down like this. Not after how far I'd come. I wouldn't let history repeat itself. I was *not* my mother. I was better than that.

I stilled.

"Ah, someone is learning fast. Don't fucking move or I will treat you like the cunt you are. Understood?" Not being able to speak out of fear that I would lose my resolve, I simply nodded.

He kissed me and I tried with everything in me not to struggle. Then as I'd hoped, he slid off of me and stood at the edge of the bed. Cracking my eyes open, I watched as he started to undo his belt buckle. I quickly surveyed the room, looking to see what I had at my disposal.

A bedside lamp sat on the nightstand only a few feet away.

Taking a few deep breaths, I forcefully lifted my right leg, hitting him between the legs and watched as he crumpled to the ground. I knew I only had seconds, so I sprung up from the bed, grabbed the bedside lamp and slammed it against his temple. Holding the split top of my dress closed, I ran.

Was he bleeding? Had I killed him?

I grabbed my clutch, not wanting to leave anything behind for him to find me. Not wanting to take a chance on the elevators, I looked for the exit signs and headed for the stairs. *Shit!* I was twenty-three floors up and wearing stilettos. Flashbacks of my seventeenth birthday flashed in my head again. Once again I was fleeing down a flight of stairs from a hotel room, running for my life.

Knowing I had only seconds to spare if I didn't kill him, I ripped off my shoes and started going down taking two, sometimes three stairs at a time. Once I got to the bottom, my heart felt as though it was going to explode, but I couldn't tell if it was adrenaline or the stairs. I opened the doors and into the smoky, crowded casino, and ran straight into the bathroom. I went to the very last stall, locked the door, leaned my back against it and fell to the ground.

Then it hit me. Wracking sobs came up my throat and I couldn't breathe. Memories from seventeen years ago filled my head. *Life repeating itself.* Feeling the bile rise at the thought, I struggled to my feet and emptied my stomach contents.

I wanted Paul.

I needed Paul.

I needed him to hold me. I needed to feel the protection that has always been the constant in his arms.

After a few minutes, I put my shoes on and exited the stall. Women looked at me, but no one said a word. What was wrong with society these days? Getting a glimpse of myself in the mirror, I looked like a whore who had just got slapped around by her pimp … I kinda was. Maybe the women thought I was only fighting with my boyfriend and it wasn't their place to help me. If they only knew what I'd just endured.

I washed my mouth out, took a deep breath and left to grab a taxi to head home to Paul. I didn't have the energy to drive myself home, and I didn't know if the john would follow me. Paul was going to be pissed when he saw me, but I needed him. I had no one else, and if I didn't tell him, I didn't know when I would sleep again.

Chapter Eighteen

Paul

I was in the middle of browsing for houses to buy when the doorbell rang. I wasn't expecting anyone this late at night. It was almost midnight for Christ sakes. I wanted to get a list of houses to look at with Andi because I was quitting S&R and would no longer be welcomed in the house I was living in. Andi would since she would still be working for the company, but that needed to change as well.

I peeked out of the dining room window and saw a taxi waiting in the street. Getting to my feet, I walked to the door and opened it as a body fell onto me.

"Andi? What the fuck?" My heart stopped the moment I realized it was her. Her beautiful brown hair was tangled, her yellow dress was ripped, and her skin was starting to bruise where there wasn't already blood from cuts. "What the fuck happened?" I asked, hugging her against my body.

"You need to pay me!" the cab driver shouted from the street.

"I'm fine. Just pay him," she whispered and stumbled past me.

"The hell you are! You need to tell me what the fuck happened. Your date did this? Where's your car?"

"Just pay him." She fell to the floor.

"Baby…"

"Go!" She began to cry.

How was I supposed to leave her crying, bleeding and hurting in the entryway while I paid for a fucking cab?

"And—"

The Cabby honked and Andi whispered against the wood floor, "Please, just do it."

I ran to *our* room, grabbed my wallet off of the dresser and bolted out of the front door, jumping over Andi in the process. After glancing at the meter, I pulled the bills from my wallet and tossed them at the driver before I ran back to her. She hadn't moved in the few seconds I was gone. I scooped her up, kicked the door shut, then sat on the couch with her in my arms and rocked her, waiting for her to tell me what the fuck had happened before I lost my fucking mind.

"Baby, you need to tell me what happened before I lose my shit."

"It was like my seventeenth birthday all over again."

Her body shook as tears soaked my chest. I held her tight against me, not knowing what else to do. I wanted to beat the ever living shit out of whoever did this to her. Who would book a date with someone to do this? A motherfucking asshole, that's who.

And I was going to find him.

"He rap—" I couldn't finish my thought as I pictured Andi being held down, a man over her…

She shook her head. "No, I got away."

I squeezed her tighter, my body relaxing a little as I sank into the couch, squeezing her harder against me. "Please tell me what happened so I can help you."

"You..." She sniffed. "You can't help me."

"We can call Mark and he can call the police, have the guy arrested."

She sprang from my lap. "Shit, I have to call Eric."

I stood, reaching for her to bring her back to me. "Eric? Who's Eric?"

Confusion flashed in her eyes as she stared back at me, not moving to my outreached hand. "N-No one. Mark can't help."

"What the fuck, Andi? What's going on?"

She sighed and rubbed her forehead. Blood transferred to her hand and she stared at it as if she didn't realize she was bleeding. "My date wasn't with a client from S&R. There's just so much you don't know."

"I'm not understanding this, Andi. You need to talk to me. Why did you have a date with someone not with S&R?" My hand was still in the air. I was hoping and praying she would take it, but she didn't. Instead, she sank to the floor and started to cry again. I followed her and crouched down so I was on the same level.

"Because my mother sold me when I seventeen."

"That doesn't make any sense, baby."

She looked up at me with tears in her eyes. I pulled her to me. I didn't care if she wanted me to. This was the woman I loved and if she didn't want to be in my arms, then she needed to speak up.

She didn't. She let me hold her, her body shaking as she cried. "I want to save them all."

"Save who?"

"The girls."

She wasn't making any sense. One minute we were talking about her almost getting raped. The next we were talking about her losing her virginity. And now we were talking about her saving women? How did they all link?

"What girls?"

"The ones like Nelly," she sobbed.

Who the fuck was Nelly?

"Baby, please. You were attacked. We need to call the cops."

She pulled back. "No!" She scrambled to her feet again. "No cops. I'm done. I won't have any more dates outside of S&R. I promise." She grabbed my head on each side, peering into my eyes as if she needed to get the point across. "I promise. I won't have any more dates outside of S&R. No cops. Please, Paul," she repeated.

"Are you in danger?" She didn't say anything. "Andi…"

She pulled back and started to pace. "Leah and Nina told me not to get mixed up with this crew. I didn't listen."

"Why?" I snapped, my hands instantly clenched.

"I wanted to help the girls."

I got it. It was similar to what I did with my self-defense classes and how I showed people—especially woman how to shoot guns properly. But the question was why? "Why baby? Why do you feel you need to put your life in danger and help them?"

She groaned and started flinging her hands as she spoke. I could tell she was starting to get frustrated. "Because women shouldn't be sold like I was when I was seventeen. We should be able to choose who we want to have sex with." She stopped pacing again, dropped her hands to her side and I caught the sight of her lips starting to quiver again. "Don't you get it?"

More tears streamed down her face and I pulled her to me again. Her head fit perfectly beneath my chin and I let her cry against my chest once more. "Aren't these girls going on a date with these men and choosing to have sex with them or not?"

"Some are. Some aren't. Some are being sold without being told."

"Like sex trafficking?" She nodded. "Baby, that's the cop's jobs. You shouldn't put yourself in danger like that."

She was silent for a long time as her crying eased. "I thought I could get through to the women. Make them quit working the streets."

"This isn't what you told me on our picnic."

"I know, but I couldn't tell you then. You would have thought I was crazy."

I groaned and shook my head. "Fuck, gorgeous. I could have lost you."

"Not a chance. I'm tougher than you think."

I sighed. "I bet you are." I leaned down and kissed her lips. She winced slightly. They were busted and tasted of copper. "We need to call the cops and tell them what happened."

She shook her head. "No cops. *They* told me that if anything happened, they would be after me. I don't want any more red flags."

"Then we're going to the range tomorrow. I'm *teaching* you how to shoot."

She laughed. "You're teaching *me* how to shoot?"

I raised my eyebrows. "Yeah. I can't tell you to quit, but I won't have my woman walking around waiting for something like this to fucking happen again and not be prepared. If you have a problem with that, then too fucking bad. Fuck, Andi, this is what I *do*!"

I was ready for her to quit, but I knew she wouldn't. She was the independent type and there were things we needed to take care of before we took that step—like getting her another job.

She stared at me for a few seconds and smiled, then winced and touched her lips as if the dry blood cracked and caused her pain. "Do I win anything if I have beginner's luck?"

How was she trying to lighten the mood right now?

I thought for a moment. "If you hit the target in the heart, you win mine forever."

She laughed. "I thought I already had yours forever?"

"Of course you do, gorgeous. Let's get you cleaned up. You've had a long night."

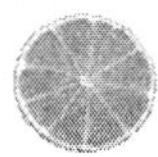

When I woke the next morning, she was already awake. I heard her on the phone as I walked by her room on the way to the kitchen. It sounded as though she'd changed her mind and had called the police to report the incident. She was telling them how it happened in room 2316 at the Wynn. I stood behind her closed bedroom door, listening, my blood boiling. But before she could hang up the phone, it struck me …

People didn't make reports over the phone.

Chapter Nineteen

Andi

"Did you bring your license?"

Paul and I were making our way into the shooting range, he was smiling like a five year old who was getting ready to walk into a candy store. I, on the other hand, wasn't so thrilled.

"Yes, but do we really have to do this? I already promised not to put myself in that position again. This is pointless." Not to mention I could already shoot the wings off a fly. Okay, maybe not that, but I was good with a gun.

Paul stopped short, turned me and grabbed my face with both hands. "I'm not taking any chances. If anything would've happened to you, I…" I saw the pain and fear in his eyes before he brought his forehead to mine and shook his head.

"Okay, let's go shoot." I had to do this for him and pretend I needed to learn how to protect myself. I was certain the only way I was able to get away from the asshole last night was because I had training. If I were a normal hooker, I probably wouldn't have been so lucky—or I'd have just let the fucker rape me.

After registering at the desk, Paul handed me a pair of ear muffs and we made our way outside. When we got to our station, there was an unloaded glock sitting at on the wood shooting table. Paul picked it up and handed it to me.

"Hold it, get familiar with the weight of it."

Trying to lighten the mood, before he got another word out I giggled. "That's what *he* said." And it worked. He started that full belly laugh that I loved hearing from him.

After we'd finished our laughing fit, he pointed to a certain part of the gun. "This is the safety. You want this on until you're ready to shoot." I nodded, letting him know I was listening. I picked up the loaded magazine, slapped it into the butt of the gun and dragged the slide back.

He stared at me. "You sure you've never done this before?"

"I watch a lot of TV?" I tried to state it as a fact, but it ended up coming out like a question.

He loaded a target onto the carrier and pressed a button, causing it to glide back into position. He took a step back. "Okay, gorgeous, come on over." With my gun still in my hands, I stood in front of him. He came up flush behind me and brought my hands up in front of me. "Hold it like this." After positioning my hands, he continued, "These peaks up here are your sights. You want your target to line up with them. Go ahead and cock it."

At the mention of *cocking it*, I rotated my hips back into his. He let out a hiss and grabbed my hips.

He leaned in, shifted a side of my earmuffs and whispered, "Careful, gorgeous, it's hard enough not to bend you over this fucking bench and fuck you with everyone watching. Watching you standing here all sexy and strong with a gun in your hand is making me hard as a fucking rock." I could feel his warm breath in my ear as he ground his now hardened dick into my ass.

I looked behind me. "It's your fault. You keep talkin' all sorts of dirty."

He chuckled. "Okay, let's focus before I do something that gets us kicked out of here for indecent exposure. Once you've *kicked the hammer* back, take aim and slowly pull the trigger back. Make sure you keep your arms stiff, tight. Keep your arms tight. The kickback can be a bitch."

I did just that, but knowing I couldn't let on that I knew what I was doing, I lazily took aim and pulled the trigger. My shot landed just outside the black rings on the target.

"Come on baby, you got this. Focus."

Hearing encouraging words from Paul was all I needed. I took my stance and lifted my gun. Practicing my shooting at the range back in D.C., I used to imagine it was Marco's face—or what I could remember from that dreadful night—plastered on the targets I shot at; now it was the face of the prick who tried to rape me.

I unloaded the entire magazine into the target, each one landing on the bullseye. As Paul had previously instructed, I flipped the safety on and lowered my glock, trying to get my breathing under control. I went stiff and froze, not remembering that Paul was standing behind me. I just blew my fucking cover. I knew it. When I turned around, Paul was gawking at me with his mouth open, trying not to smile.

"That has got to be the sexiest fucking thing I have *ever* seen. I had a feeling you'd rock this shit."

I set my gun down on the table, walked over to him and placed a chaste kiss to his lips. "All right, sexy, let's see whatcha got."

Walking past me, he gave my ass a little swat. "Watch and learn, baby, watch and learn." Letting out a sigh of relief, I cursed myself. It was getting harder and harder to lie to him. I loved him. I didn't want to lie. I didn't want to hurt him. After taking a few more rounds each, we called it a day. Although I knew what I was doing, Paul was an amazing teacher. If Gabe was like him, they were going to be expanding the self-defense classes sooner rather than later.

Paul threw an arm around my waist and pulled me in. "Let's get home, gorgeous. After what I just witnessed, I wanna get home and love hard on my girl." He kissed me senseless, leaving me breathless …

Again.

Just through the garage door, Paul spun me around and grabbed me by the waist and hoisted me over his shoulder giving my ass a slap.

"I think we both need to unwind tonight, baby. I see a bottle of tequila, two shot glasses and you naked in the near future."

"Oh, so you're a fortune teller now?"

He plopped me down on the kitchen countertop and made his way over to the cabinet he always kept stocked with liquor. "What'll it be tonight, gorgeous?"

"Um … Jose?"

"Good choice." He winked at me and I blushed. I wasn't sure I would ever tire of the way he had that effect on me.

Drip.

Drip.

Drip.

After setting the bottle next to my thigh, he made his way to the other side of the kitchen and pulled out two shot glasses and the table salt just before grabbing a lime from the fruit basket. When he turned and caught me staring, he let out a chuckle.

"What? You have done tequila shots before, right?"

I hopped off the counter and made my way over to him, grabbed the lime to slice it into wedges and repeated the words he'd said to me at the firing range. "Watch and learn, baby, watch and learn."

Then I grabbed all of the contents out of his hands except one of the shot glasses and turned to pour myself some Cuervo while Paul made his way to the other side of the counter and leaned on his elbows to watch. Knowing he was watching me, I gave the area between my thumb and pointer finger on my hand a slow, long lick with the flat of my tongue and grinned when I heard him groan.

I sprinkled the salt on the spot I'd licked, grabbed a lime wedge with the same hand and my shot of Jose with the other, and gave him my best devious smile. "Cheers." I licked my hand and tossed back the tequila just before lifting the lime to my mouth and sucking it.

Paul stood up and slowly walked over to me. The look in his eyes caused the junction between my legs to spasm. He looked like a wild cat closing in on his prey. "Oh no, no, no, gorgeous. You did that all wrong. Who showed you how to do a tequila shot? Let's correct this, shall we?"

I nodded and bit my lip, stifling a squeal as he grabbed my waist and hoisted me back up on the countertop. Pulling the strap of my tank top down my arm with my bra strap, his eyes met mine briefly before he lowered his to the side to untwist the top to the salt shaker with one hand and empty it onto the granite countertop before pouring himself a shot. When he moved his face back into my line of sight, he was smiling.

"As I've said before, the correct way …" He fused his mouth to mine causing me to moan just before he disconnected, placed a lime wedge between my lips and whispered in my ear, "Is to take the shot …"

Lowering his head, he ran his tongue along the skin at my collar bone. Goosebumps spread across my entire body and I knew if he kept this up, I was going to end up leaving a wet spot on the counter from how turned on he was making me. I closed my eyes and tipped my head to the side to give him more access.

His lips left my neck and a hand came up and rubbed the coarse salt where his mouth had been. He leaned back down near my ear, and while placing the shot glass between my tits, he whispered, "…off someone else's skin."

I could feel the abrasion of the salt against my skin as Paul licked it from my neck. He cupped both of my breasts and lightly ran his thumb pads over my now oversensitive nipples while taking the shot glass from in between them with his mouth. He threw his head back to help the alcohol slide down the back of his throat before catching the empty shot glass between our bodies and setting it beside us. He then reached up, grabbed my face with both hands as he took the lime from between my lips and gave it a quick suck before he let that fall between us before he claimed my lips.

"Your way is *much* better," I panted.

"I don't like this," Paul groaned, crossing his arms as he watched me apply the final touches of my makeup.

"We've gone over this. It's an S&R date."

"It's too soon."

"I'll be fine." I screwed the cap on the tub of my mascara and threw it on the counter. I started to walk down the hall to the kitchen.

"I'm going with you."

I threw my head back and laughed. "You're not going with me on my date."

"Yes, I am." He was talking nonsense.

I grabbed my purse off the kitchen table, needing to leave. "Don't be ridiculous. I'll be fine. It's an S&R date, not a top secret date that I will never go on again."

So … that may or may not be true. I still needed more research. I'd had one date that ended badly. I didn't know who Martinez was and I needed to find more girls who could get me closer to meeting him.

After the incident at the Wynn, I'd called the secure line for the FBI and reported it. I'd needed to let Eric know. I needed to report my findings, and if the man had died then the bureau could handle it since I was undercover and my DNA and prints were all over the room. I was also probably caught on camera fleeing the scene.

"Do you have your gun?" Paul looked down at my purse in my hands as I opened the front door. We bought me one at the range before we left. There was no way he was letting that slide even though I already had one in my room.

"Yes, sexy." I kissed him quickly before walking out the front door. Paul grabbed his keys and started to walk toward the garage. "Where are you going?"

"Going on your date."

I put a hand on my hip. "You're serious?"

"As a fucking heart attack."

I knew I wasn't going to be able to stop him, so I rolled my eyes, got in my car and backed out of the driveway. When I pulled into the parking lot of the restaurant, Paul parked beside me. I glared at him and shook my head.

"Gorgeous," he called out.

"You better stay at the bar," I whispered and kept walking, not wanting to bring attention to us. I didn't want to stop in case my date was already inside the restaurant and could see. I wasn't at a hotel because my date was only for lunch. I'd never had a lunch date before; maybe he thought it would end with a nooner. Guess we'd find out. I was getting good at turning them down for sex, minus Martinez's guy who clearly got off raping women.

I walked into the Mexican food restaurant and to the hostess stand.

"I'm meeting a Mr. Sanchez for lunch," I explained.

She looked at her reservation list on her computer. "Yes, we have your reservation, but he hasn't arrived. It says to go ahead and seat you."

"Perfect," I replied.

I looked over my shoulder and gave Paul a tight smile before following the hostess to the back corner of the restaurant. As we walked, I noticed the restaurant had minimal people, but yet she took me to the farthest corner of the restaurant. I didn't think much of it. Mr. Sanchez had probably requested a quiet table where we could be alone and he wouldn't get caught with an escort.

I sat with my back to the wall, facing the bar. I was able to see Paul and would see Mr. Sanchez when he arrived. I didn't want to admit it but having Paul there put me at ease. I wasn't in a hotel room and I would never be in one again with a client, but having my man there was like having backup even if I had my gun sitting in my clutch purse that was on the table.

The busser came over and left a glass of water, a basket of tortilla chips and a dish of salsa. I caught the gaze of Paul. I expected him to be sipping a Coke and tequila, but he too was drinking water. He winked at me and I blushed. I couldn't help it. No matter how mad I was that he'd insisted on coming with me to my date, I still loved him with all of my heart. I knew he was only doing it because he loved me. I couldn't imagine what would have happened if that man had raped me. It would have destroyed everything we'd built. I don't think I would have been able to survive it, let alone the touch of a man again.

"Preciosa." *Gorgeous.*

I looked up and into the same eyes I looked into every day in the mirror and blinked, unable to say anything. My mouth went dry. My heart stopped beating. I was certain I couldn't breathe.

He unbuttoned his suit jacket and slid into his chair in front of me. "Have we met before?"

We had.

I'd raised him from the moment he was born until I went running for my life.

My gaze flicked to Paul's. I needed him. I needed him to breathe because I couldn't. This wasn't happening. What did I do? How did I tell the man sitting across from me that he was my brother?

"That's not possible. I know all the *whores* in this town."

He didn't recognize me, but I was sure of it. This *was* my brother. My gaze flicked down to his hand that was running along the condensation of the ice water. Along the inside of his palm was the mark from the cigarette burn my mother gave him when he was four and she'd used him as an ashtray.

I smiled tightly and took a sip of my water, trying to think of what to do. He'd hired me as an escort. Obviously I wasn't going to—*gross!*

"So tell me, Andi," he leaned forward, crossed his hands on the table and looked into my eyes, "what do you think gives you the right to disobey my orders?"

My head tilted to the side in confusion. "Your orders?"

He smirked. "You don't know who I am?"

"Bryce," I whispered.

He leaned back in his chair. "Well, that's funny. Usually, the whores I fuck are the only ones who know my first name."

"I—"

"Which one of my whores is running her mouth, Andi? Huh?" He hit the table with his fist and I jumped. Paul looked over and I shook my head slightly.

"I don't know what you mean."

He leaned forward again. "I'll ask you again. What gives you the right to disobey my orders?"

"What orders?" I asked, scrunching my eyebrows.

"Come on, Andi. Don't play stupid. I know some of you whores are stupid, but you don't look like one of them. Jasmine told me you were smart. Let's act like it."

My head cocked back. "Jasmine?"

"Okay, so you are stupid." He laughed.

My gaze flicked to Paul and he was staring at us. I wanted to motion for him to come sit with us, be my back-up. I felt like my head was spinning. I was talking about one thing and Bryce was talking about another—and then it clicked.

"You're Martinez?"

"Ding, ding, ding. We have a winner, folks!"

When I'd left the hotel twelve years ago, I thought I would return to the trailer park to save Bryce, but forty-eight hours later I'd learned that Tony took him and my mother, only to never be heard of again—until now. I never knew why.

As I stared into the honey eyes that were similar to mine, I knew there was no saving this man I didn't know. It was too late. Even though he had my eyes, his weren't warm and inviting. They were cold and dark, as if they didn't care if he lived or died on any given day. Tony had raised him and made him the man he was today. The boy I was raising would never treat a woman the way he was speaking to me. He would never call women whores. Would never order a woman around. He would be more like Paul—more like Seth even.

I gave Paul one final look and then I acted. Whatever happened beyond this point was out of my control. I had a gun and if I had to shoot my own blood, then that was what I was going to do. Paul raised his eyebrows and his gaze lowered to my hand as it went inside my clutch. I saw him reach behind his back as I pulled my gun out and stood.

"FBI. Get on the fucking ground, hands behind you back." I pointed my gun at Bryce and he laughed.

Paul stood with a look of confusion on his face as his gaze went back and forth between my brother and me.

"Get on the fucking ground!" I repeated, the gun in both of my hands as I pointed it at him.

Two big goons ran in behind Bryce. Paul pulled his gun and pointed it at them. They skidded to a stop and drew their own guns.

"All right, everyone needs to calm the fuck down," Bryce interjected, trying to get everyone to lower their weapons. People in the restaurant were screaming and running for the doors.

"Bryce, you're not running the show. Get on the fucking ground. I'm not going to ask you again!"

Bryce laughed again, grabbing his belly as though he couldn't contain himself. "I don't take orders from whores!"

Reaching into my purse, I grabbed my wallet and pulled my badge out. "Does this look like I'm fucking around?" I shouted, showing him my credentials that accompanied the gold plated badge.

The sound of guns cocking followed by *pop, pop, pop* sent the room into a frenzy. Pain tore through the flesh of my right arm, causing me to lose my balance as I saw Paul rush Bryce. He tackled him, sending them both crashing into the wood table. Fists flew as Paul connected his with Bryce's jaw and I scrambled to my feet. Paul flipped him over, pulling Bryce's arms behind his back with a little more force than necessary.

With the barrel of the gun against the back of his head, I repeated myself again to Bryce, "Hands behind your back."

Paul held him as I looked for Bryce's guys. They were lying motionless in puddles of blood where they stood before.

"You shot them?" I asked Paul.

"They shot at you first."

I looked down at my arm, blood trickled down and onto the butt of the gun I was aiming at Bryce on the floor. Sirens could be heard in the distance and I knew I would be fine. "Thank you."

"When were you going to tell me you were FBI?"

I sighed. "I couldn't."

"Why? You told me other things."

"I'm undercover."

He gave a sarcastic chuckle. "Is your name even Andi?"

I was tired of lying. I was tired of lying to everyone. I'd been lying for twelve years. And most of all, I loved Paul. I loved him so much. I wanted to spend forever with him. I wanted to hear him call me by my real name—groan my real name when he made love to me. Tell the *real me* that he loved me.

"You'll want to hear this too," I said to Bryce as I nudged his side with my foot. He snorted as if I lost my mind, but turned his head as if curiosity got the best of him.

"My name's Joselyn Marquez."

Chapter Twenty

Joselyn

Realization flashed across Bryce's face the moment I uttered my real name and then it seemed as though it vanished. Paul was still looking at me as though his heart was breaking in two. Everything was a disaster. It was the wrong timing for all of it to go down. I never in my wildest dreams thought I would be reunited with my brother and arresting him because he was the ringleader in the sex trafficking case I was undercover in. I wanted to kick and scream at the thought of how this had happened. How he fucking grew up to become *this* man.

I'd never thought Paul would find out that I was undercover like this. I knew eventually the case would come to a close. I never knew when, though. He stared at me as if he didn't know me from the next cop in the sea of them buzzing around the crime scene.

Before I could tell Paul that we'd talk at home and everything would be okay, the local police department was rushing in and both Bryce and Paul were handcuffed. I explained that it was Bryce who needed to be handcuffed, not Paul, and then immediately reached for my cell to call Eric.

After explaining on the secure line that I needed to get the local division involved to apprehend Bryce, they told me to *hang tight* while they contacted Eric and the local bureau. Paul was questioned by the local PD, my arm was patched up by the paramedics and then I was pulled aside by the head of the local FBI division.

"Agent Marquez, I'm Agent Reigles. Agent Green called me. If you want to come with me, we'll take Martinez in and question him down in our office."

I nodded and gave Paul one final look before we left for their headquarters. I wanted to tell him more, but he was being asked to make his own statement of what happened.

I was certain everything would be okay once we met back home.

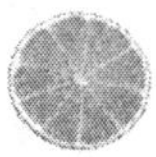

In the short ride down to the bureau, Agent Reigles and I didn't speak much. We couldn't talk about the case and I was glad. I wondered if I should tell anyone that Bryce was my brother. I wondered if *he* was going to say he was my brother—if he understood he was even my brother. There was no way he didn't remember … Right? There were so many things I wanted to ask him and he was sitting right behind me. After over a decade, my flesh and blood was finally in the same car as me and I couldn't speak to him. Couldn't hug him, kiss him, tell him that I missed him.

What had Tony done to him?

We pulled into the parking lot and escorted Bryce into the building. I was starting to get sick to my stomach. Could I do this? Could I act as if Bryce was only another criminal I'd arrested several times? I wanted to ask him every question but the ones pertaining to the investigation. I didn't care anymore about the case. I wanted to know what had happened the night of my birthday when I didn't return home. I wanted to know what had happened the next day, the next week, the next month, year—years even. What had happened to our mother? Why was he was now Bryce Martinez and not Bryce Marquez?

Instead, as we sat him down in the black metal chair behind a white metal table under the florescent lighting in the small room, Reigles gave me the lead and again, like everything else, I faked it.

"Comfortable?" I asked motioning to the cuffs.

"Are these really necessary?" He raised his arms from his lap.

"Let's see how this goes. Your men shot me and my arm's a little sore." Really the cuffs weren't necessary, the door was locked, but for some reason a part of me felt as if I released him from them, it would show special treatment. It was ridiculous, but I needed him to be like a criminal and not my brother.

He chuckled. "They saw a gun—"

I slapped the table with my right hand, causing pain to radiate through my arm. "You don't know what they were thinking!"

He rolled his eyes. Either we were both really good at faking it or he didn't know I was his sister.

Did Tony brainwash him?

"Now, Martinez, let's cut the shit. You hired me today to scare me because the other night a john in your company tried to rape me—"

"You have no proof I'm involved."

"You said, and I quote, 'What gives you the right to disobey my orders?'."

"That could mean anything, preciosa."

"Don't call me that!"

"Touchy, touchy!" He laughed.

I looked over at Agent Reigles and sighed. I realized that I didn't have proof that Bryce was involved, yet he was Martinez and I knew first hand that he was running the streets because the girls had mentioned him by name. If I had known that I was meeting him for lunch, I would have recorded the conversation with him and gotten my proof. Instead, it was my word against his. As I stared into those fucking eyes that matched mine, I realized I was fucked.

"Your girl Jasmine and I have become close you know. We've played craps at the Palazzo together."

He leaned back in his chair, spread his legs wide and smiled. "Agent Marquez, I run an escort business similar to Saddles & Racks. It's no different from what you do. It's not my fault when you took a date from my company to make extra money on the side that that guy took it too far." He looked under the table as if to look at my body. I was still in my dress from our date and I closed my eyes, trying to stomach the fact that my *brother* was doing this. "I don't blame him. In fact, it's my understanding you killed him. I was wondering why you weren't being charged for murder. Now I know. So, Jasmine did her job. She hooked you and got you under my payroll."

I laughed. "Bryce … Can I call you Bryce? I feel as if I've known you since you've been *born*." I was done fucking around.

He chuckled. "You can call me whatever you want."

"Bryce, I met with your girls for drinks one night, and one mentioned her best friend, Nelly was sold by you."

He *tsked.* "They're just whores running their mouths."

"That's funny because I have them in my pocket ready to come forward. I told them that once I had you, I just needed them and they were quick to turn on you."

"That doesn't make sense because they would have just led you to me."

"See ... I thought that, too. But you scared them and they thought you were going to scare me." I laughed. "*You* thought you were going to scare me. Do you always set your girls up first with rape dates? Is that how it works? Rape them first so they do whatever you want and if they don't then you sell them?"

He was silent and I continued before he asked for a lawyer. I knew it was coming because I was right. I could feel it in my bones. That was how he worked. "How many have you sold, Bryce? How did this start? When did this start? When did you move to Vegas? Did Tony do this to you?"

His gaze darted to mine at the mention of Tony. "How do you know about Tony?" he asked.

I rubbed the bridge of my nose with a sigh and took a few moments before I spoke. This was the make it or break it moment that I needed to determine if we were on the same page. I needed to know if he knew I was his sister or not.

"Have you ever wanted a Dalmatians plantation?" His eyes became big, but he didn't say anything and I continued and quoted the first quote I could think of from *101 Dalmatians*. "But I am, just the same. I'm so hungry I could eat a … a whole elephant."

He stilled and stared me straight in the eyes. If he didn't know before, he knew now. I'd always called our mother Cruella. It wasn't only because she was evil—she was, but it was because we watched that movie on repeat because it was the only thing we had to watch for entertainment. We knew almost every line. I'd chosen that line in particular because on several occasions we did go hungry growing up.

"Are you okay?" Agent Reigles asked.

"Yeah. Sorry, I never got to eat at lunch since this was supposed to be my lunch date." I laughed, trying to brush off the hint I was giving Bryce. "So Bryce—"

"I'm the middle man," he blurted.

I pulled my head back in confusion. "What?"

"You're right. Tony made me do it."

"Who's Tony?" Reigles asked.

"My father," Bryce replied.

I stared at him. "Your … father?"

He nodded. "Do you want my life story or what?"

"Does it pertain to the case?" Reigles asked. I wanted to reach over and cover her mouth with my hand. I wanted his entire life story. I wanted it all!

"I think most of it does." He nodded. "It started when I was eight." He looked me square in the eyes. He knew. This was it. This was the moment I'd been waiting for.

"And you're willing to talk without a lawyer present?"

"Let the man talk!" I spat. *Jesus!*

Bryce laughed. "I've been waiting for the day I could take down my father."

Me too! "I think we can remove the cuffs now. Get you some water." I stood and started to remove the cuffs as Agent Reigles left the room to get the water. It was the first time I was trying to fight back tears. This was my brother. I wanted to wrap him in my arms and hug him. I didn't care *who* he was and what he'd been doing for the last twelve years. I'd missed him.

Reigles returned with a bottle of water and Bryce took a few sips. "The night of my sister's seventeenth birthday, all I wanted was cake. We never got treats. I was eight and thought that we'd at least have a cake. Instead, our mother sent her out with my dad. At the time, I didn't know he was my dad. I don't think she knew he was my father either because he wasn't her dad. Anyway, she never came back. To this day, I don't know what happened to her."

I pulled everything from within me to show no emotions as he stared directly at me and told the story.

"That night, my dad came into our trailer and beat my mom. I'd thought that he'd beaten her to death, but I was too young to know for sure, so I left her in her room. The next day he returned and took us. She wasn't dead, but we left and never returned. I thought for sure my sister was dead and I cried. I cried for days, but never in front of my mother and that man. I didn't want him to beat me like he beat her, I only wanted my sister because she was my best friend. But she never returned to get me."

I stood, causing the metal chair to screech in the process. I was about to lose my shit and become a blubbering mess. I should have returned that night and taken him with me. I had enough money for two bus tickets. Seth could have taken us both in. Instead, my actions caused my brother to become a criminal.

"He filed some papers and changed my last name to Martinez. Growing up he forced me to do things that I never wanted to do. Steal this, beat him up, fuck her. It escalated each time. Eventually, we moved here from Miami and started picking up the prostitutes working the streets of Vegas, or the Weekend Warriors who fly in just on the weekends to have a good time. Those are the best ones because it's harder to know they're missing.

"Anyway, my mother killed herself three years ago. She left a suicide note and confessed that Tony was my father, so it's only fitting he has me running his business for him."

"How did…?"

"She overdosed on oxy. She said the pain of losing her daughter for selling her at seventeen was eating her alive and it was too much for her to take. She was tired of living under Tony and his orders."

"And you still think it's okay to sell women?"

"I don't have a choice."

"Why not come to the police?"

"I'd still end up in prison."

"But you'll be doing the right thing. Think about your mother. Think about your sister."

He stared at me. "Can I make a deal?"

I stared back. "What kind of deal?"

"I can't save my mother, but in hopes that my *sister's* still alive I want to make a plea in exchange for Tony. I'll work with you to bring him down."

Chapter Twenty-One

Paul

Before I could speak to Andi ... Joselyn ... Whatever her name was, the police rushed in. It was a whirlwind. At first I was handcuffed until she explained the situation and then I was asked to go down to make a statement of what happened. Then I was told to not tell anyone because Andi ... *Joselyn* was still undercover.

I didn't understand why. I thought she'd caught the guy. Why else would she pull her gun on him? Why would they shoot at her? And why did she reveal her real name?

Usually, I would go to Gabe and talk everything out with him, but I couldn't tell him that I was just in a shootout with two thugs, a pimp, and my FBI girlfriend. I'd thought his situation with Major Dick was crazy, but I believed mine was the icing on the cake and I couldn't even tell him.

Wasn't that some shit?

So I went to the liquor store, bought a bottle of tequila and went home to wait for whatever the fuck her name was. I wasn't sure why I was mad at her—but I was. I was questioning if it was all even real between us or if it was all an act. I half expected her shit to be packed and moved out by the time I arrived home. But when I pulled in and peeked in her room, everything was the same. I showered and changed into shorts and then broke open the bottle of agave goodness.

I was halfway through the bottle, watching ESPN and almost forgetting that I'd killed two men—something I hadn't done since Afghanistan when Andi ... *Joselyn* walked in.

"Hey," she greeted.

"Hey," I slurred.

"Are you doing okay?" she asked, setting her purse down on the coffee table and sitting next to me. I tensed and so did she. "You're mad?"

"Of course I am!" I shouted and stood. *Well, stumbled.*

"You're drunk."

"And you're an FBI agent. Are you going to arrest me now?"

"Why are you being an asshole?"

I swayed for a few seconds and then sat on the coffee table, unable to stand any longer from the alcohol in my system. "Do you know what happened today?" I snapped, jerking my head up a little too fast. I was referring to the fact I'd killed two men.

She stood. "Do *you* know what happened today?"

"I learned that you've been lying to me this entire time."

"I only lied to you about my occupation, *Paul*."

I laughed and shook my head. "Are you sure about that, *gorgeous*?"

"What the fuck does that mean?"

"I've been sitting here for hours questioning everything."

She sat back down and reach for me, but I slid a few feet from her so she couldn't touch me. "Why?" she asked.

I chuckled. "You were placed here by the FBI and then you struck up a relationship with me. I've replayed everything over and over in my head, but I don't know what's real and what's not."

"Everything between us is real."

"Except your name."

"Yes, except my name."

I looked directly into her eyes, wanting to know the one hundred percent truth about my next question. "What about your seventeenth birthday?"

"It was all true. What I felt for you and what I told you was true. I fell in love with you. If you can't grasp that, then I don't know what else to tell you. I've had a long and emotional day." She stood and so did I.

"*You* had an emotional day? You caught the guy you were after. I saved your fucking life. And all I got when you walked in the door was a hey."

"Sex—"

"No!" I wasn't sure if it was the tequila, my heart, the fact that she'd lied to me or that I had killed two men, but I was angry and I was angry at her and I couldn't hold my tongue once I started. "Don't sexy me, Andi … *Joselyn*, whatever the fuck your name is. I killed two fucking men today and I can't even talk to my best friend about it. Fuck, I can't even talk to you about it because you weren't here. Now I get a fucking hey. Well, fuck your hey. See, this is why I don't date. Women and their fucking games—"

"What games are you talking about? I'm not playing games!"

"You are with my heart!"

"I'm not playing games with your heart."

"You pretended to love me."

"Is that really what you think?" She crossed her arms over her chest.

"Yes."

She stared at me for what felt like an eternity. I didn't know why I said the things coming from my mouth. The more I said them, the more I knew they weren't true, but I felt like hurting her.

She reached down and grabbed her purse from the coffee table. I watched her wipe tears from her cheek. I didn't even know I'd made her cry. I wanted to reach out and pull her to me, tell her I was sorry, that I didn't mean any of it.

But before I could utter anything she spoke as she reached the front door.

"Everything I ever told you, everything I ever felt for you, was real. You're the only man I've ever loved and on my seventeenth birthday my mother not only sold my virginity, but I ran away from home and left my eight year old brother behind. Today the man I arrested was my brother. After everything that happened today, I'm staying undercover because he's only the middle man. I'll have the bureau retrieve my stuff in the morning. Take care of yourself, Paul." Before I could get to her, she was in her car and backing out of the driveway.

And I was too drunk to chase after her.

Chapter Twenty-Two

Joselyn

The green light blurred as I stared at it behind my tears. It was as if it was raining and my windshield was covered with raindrops, but it was my eyes. I hadn't cried so hard since—*ever.*

The night of my seventeenth birthday I'd cried, but my tears weren't all at once. And just the other night when I'd almost gotten raped … but it wasn't nearly as painful. After this, I might as well just throw my heart out the window and run it over with my car.

I was done.

There was no point to living anymore.

Bryce was alive. He was going to help the FBI bring down Tony. My mother was dead, and Paul had just taken my heart and smashed it with the fucking tequila bottle he was currently drowning in, repeatedly slicing it with the shattered glass.

The car honked behind me and I took off. My phone in my purse buzzed. I knew who was calling. Only a handful of people had the number, so I didn't bother to pick it up. There was no point in answering. I didn't want to fight with him anymore. I'd said what I needed to say. I was going to a hotel for the night, and in the morning

I would let the bureau know I needed a new place to live.

It was better off we ended because we couldn't work out. I was getting deeper into this investigation. For me, it was all about taking down criminals. For Paul, it was all about the money and having fun. I didn't think my heart could take knowing Paul went on dates with other women anymore.

I was going to go back to my life where it was nothing but work. That was where I thrived. If I hadn't mixed business with pleasure, I'd probably have been more prepared on my date with the john who tried to rape me and also the one with Bryce. Paul was clouding my judgment and I needed to focus on the reason I came to Vegas.

But I still loved him …

Fuck, I still loved him.

Maybe after the investigation things would be different. I needed time. Time to do my job.

I drove to the south end of town to get a hotel. I didn't have any clothes or toiletries, but I'd been in this situation before. Funny thing was, I was dressed like a hooker again.

The next morning I called the secure line and told them I needed a new place to live. For the next two days, I stayed with Leah. I told her that things got weird with my *roommate* and she didn't ask many questions. Paul tried calling me a few times, but I didn't answer. I couldn't. I couldn't hear his voice because I was certain I would die inside. He texted me a few times, telling me he loved me and to come home, but I didn't text back.

My stuff was moved into a new house in two days. We worked fast at the FBI apparently and there was always a vacant house in Vegas. By day three I was in my own three bedroom house—lonely and missing Paul like crazy.

The following Monday, I was brought into the local Vegas division for a meeting with Eric and Agent Reigles about where we wanted the case to go. I wasn't happy about being undercover still. I wanted to go back to D.C. I missed Seth and I couldn't wait to see him again. It felt like ages since I'd last seen him or even heard his voice.

Knowing that Bryce was the middle man who was going to help us take down Tony was the only thing keeping me strong in this entire shit show.

While I sipped on my coffee, waiting for Eric to show, my cell rang again. It was Paul. I wanted to talk to him, but I couldn't. This was for the best. One day we'd both move on. I'd go back to D.C. and everything would return to normal.

Normal.

Unhappy, but normal.

"It's good to see you again." Eric smiled, walking into the boardroom and bringing me out of my thoughts.

I nodded with a tight smile. "You, too, Eric." Agent Reigles followed him in and the three of us sat around the wood table with our notepads, sipping coffee. "Good work, by the way."

I blushed. "Thank you."

"All right, let's get down to business. It's my understanding this

Martinez guy wants a plea." I nodded. "Are we certain we can trust him? Are your leads good?"

I stared at him for a moment, trying to remember codes and procedures in my head as I came up with a plan on the fly. This was my brother. I still had that instinct to protect him. I knew once everything was said and done, he would go to jail—probably for a long time, but if I was able to do anything to help him, I was going to try.

"Joss?"

I shook my head as if I had cobwebs in it. "Sorry." I flicked my gaze to Agent Reigles and then back to Agent Green. They were both about to know me a whole lot better. "Eric, you've known me for how long?" He shook his head as though he couldn't remember.

"Three … four years?" I asked.

"About that."

"There's something you need to know about me. Please let me finish before you stop me because I have a plan."

"Okay." He nodded.

"Agent Reigles, this may sound familiar, but please let me finish." She nodded as well.

I took a deep breath, took a sip of coffee, and then another deep breath before I began. "When I was seventeen, my mother sold my virginity …" My gaze flicked to Agent Reigles as she gasped.

I proceeded to tell them the entire story up until Bryce wanted the plea deal. "There's no one more determined than I am to bring this asshole Tony down. To answer your question, we can trust him. He's my brother, but I didn't find out until the day I arrested him. I didn't even know it was him until I arrested him." They stared at me as I continued talking. "I was thinking that the only way for this to really work is to partner me up this time. Send me with someone I can trust. But not with a female. We need a male."

"A male?" Eric asked.

"Yeah, I want you to bring in someone for a special unit. Seth McKenna is a detective with the DCPD. I trust him with my life. I want him as my partner."

"We can provide you with a partner, Joss," Agent Reigles stated.

"I know, but he also knows Bryce. If you want this case to be solved, it's in your best interest to put the two people on it who would want it solved the most."

Eric thought for a few seconds. I knew that the FBI partnered other agencies with different tasks forces all the time. It wasn't unheard of to bring in outside help. Seth had the credentials to have been able to become FBI before I did. He just liked solving murders and working the streets. I knew going undercover and helping me with Bryce wouldn't be a hesitation.

"All right. Let's get him out here."

Chapter Twenty-Three

Paul

She'd left and walked out the door with my heart.

I knew I'd been a complete asshole the moment I woke up on the couch, my head pounding and the tequila bottle staring me in the face. I'd tried calling her over and over and over, but she never picked up the phone.

Rolling off the couch, I stood and walked down the hall to her empty room. I half expected her to be in there, but she wasn't. I'd seriously fucked up. If it weren't for my fucking mouth, she'd be sleeping in *our* bed and I'd be making us breakfast. So what if her name was Joselyn and not Andi—at least Joselyn's a girl's name. A gorgeous name; as gorgeous as she was. And she worked for the FBI. Well, If she didn't, we would have never met. I was a fucking idiot. I'd let the best thing that had ever happened to me walk out the door. And worst of all, I had no one to talk to about it.

I kept trying her cell over and over, but she never picked up. I just wanted to tell her I was sorry. We'd had a fight. People fight. We'd had a fucked up, crazy day and we needed to be with each other—I needed her.

She never answered. Instead, like she'd said, a moving company came and took her stuff. They packed up her room as if none of it mattered. As if *we* hadn't matter.

Well, fuck that shit.

If what she'd said was true and *everything* we had together was real, then she wasn't getting away that easy. I refused to love for this reason, and now that I'd opened my heart to love again, I wasn't going to lose it—*again.*

I wanted what Gabe and Autumn had. I wanted to feel what I saw on their faces—the love they felt when everything around them didn't matter because they had each other. I wanted to know what it felt like to have the family I'd always wanted. To have the child I'd once lost.

We all had our flaws, and I didn't care about Joselyn's. I knew she worried that I cared about her past, but I still loved her. Her past didn't define her future. It was how she'd overcome it that made her who she was now.

I just had to prove it.

As the moving truck pulled away, I followed it. Joselyn said she was staying undercover. I didn't know if that meant in Vegas, but I had an idea. It also involved me quitting S&R and stat.

Add stalking to my resume. Or creeper—whatever. Joselyn was either going to arrest me after what I was about to do, or have hot monkey sex with me. I was obviously hoping for the latter. I wasn't used to the whole dating for real thing, so if this went south, Gabe was going to need to bail me out of jail.

After I'd followed the truck, I wrote down the address. It was a house still in Vegas so I knew Joselyn was staying in town. I called Mark on my way to the jewelry store where I was going to buy her the biggest diamond I could afford. I didn't care we were broken up and she'd moved out. I loved her.

Mark was pissed he was losing another one of his escorts. In fact, he'd said he was losing his best escort. What could I say—I knew how to fuck. Joselyn hadn't seen my best moves yet because she was only getting into her groove, but if she said yes … oh, if she said yes, she'd know why I'd had so many dates and repeat clients.

After the jewelry store, I went home to pack and wait.

That was the worst part.

Waiting for the right time to make my move felt like torture.

My entire house was packed in boxes and my *Jeep* held my suitcase. I told Mark that I'd be out by the end of the month. If what I was about to do didn't work out, then I would find a place of my own.

I was sitting out front of the house that I'd seen the moving truck deliver all of Joselyn's belongings to and I was beginning to get nervous.

I was starting to second guess my plan.

I wanted this.

I wanted her.

I wanted her more than anything in the world.

But what if she didn't want me?

Taking a deep breath, I opened the *Jeep* door and got out. I needed to find out my fate. My heart was racing, my palms were sweaty, and the damn velvet box with the two-carat, solitaire cushion diamond on a platinum band was burning a hole in my jeans pocket. I'd never been so nervous in my life. War wasn't this nerve racking and that was crazy to think about. Going into combat, you had no time to over-think, but the last few days, that's all I'd done.

I walked up to the front door, my suitcase in tow, and rang the doorbell. I hadn't seen her for almost a week and it had been the longest week of my entire life. I hadn't eaten. I'd canceled my classes at the gym. Gabe and Autumn had tried to see me, but I'd told them I was sick. I didn't want to see anyone until I knew what the future held for me and the girl who'd come into my life like a wrecking ball.

She opened the door with a smile spread across her face and then it fell—so did mine along with my heart.

"Are you going to let me in or are you going to leave me standing on the porch?" It was the same line she'd said to me the first time we'd met. It was my only saving grace.

She looked down at my suitcase and didn't say anything, so I moved to the next part of the plan and just walked in. "What are you doing?" she asked.

"I'm barging into your life, gorgeous, just like you barged into mine. You don't get to walk out of mine when we have a fight."

"We had more than a fight." She closed the door, but I was on the inside. This was a good sign.

"Did we?"

She nodded. "We broke up."

"Why?"

She stared at me. "Because you didn't think that I really loved you."

I reached into my pocket and pulled out the ring box and got down on one knee. "This will answer my question once and for all now, won't it?"

Her eyes became huge and her hand covered her mouth. Tears pricked her eyes and she uttered the words I didn't want her to say. "Stop."

"What?"

She removed her hand. "Stop," she whispered.

My head hung. I couldn't move even if I wanted to. I'd thought her tears were tears of joy and she was on the verge of saying yes. I had no idea that her tears were because she wanted me to stop. I started to stand, but it was no use; I had no energy. All of it was consumed by everything in me trying not to break down and cry. No one had ever seen me weak and no one ever would—not even Joselyn. She didn't deserve it. I stuffed the ring back into my pocket and stayed on my knees.

"It's not that I don't want to marry you," she continued, "but I can't." My head shot up. She knelt down to my level and we were eye-to-eye. "I'm undercover. I can't get married. Plus, how would it look when two escorts got married?"

"One escort," I clarified.

"One?"

"I quit."

"You quit?"

I nodded. "I don't want any of that anymore, gorgeous. I just want you."

She looked up at the ceiling not saying anything for a long time. "Then we'll figure something out because I want you, too."

"Is that a yes then? Will you marry me?"

She smiled and nodded, more tears in her eyes. "Yes!"

I acted fast, scooping her up off the floor. It had been over a week since I'd tasted her skin. I was about to find out what this new house was made of because I wasn't going to be able to contain myself once I was buried deep inside my *fiancé*.

A frame shattered on the wood floor as I pushed her back against the wall. Our mouths didn't break from savoring each other at the crash. I missed the feel of our lips together, of our tongue mixing and of her—just her.

I brought her T-shirt over her head and tossed it onto the floor then cupped her breast in my hand roughly. Maybe too roughly; I wasn't sure. I was on fire.

"I missed you so fucking much," I confessed against her lips.

"I missed you, too," she panted.

My hand slipped down into the waistband of her shorts and straight into her panties. She was dripping wet. "Jesus, baby."

I slid and dropped to my knees, unbuttoned her jean shorts, and pulled them and her panties down her legs. I could smell her arousal and my mouth watered. Hooking one leg over my shoulder, I spread her pussy and she glistened. I groaned as she moaned and tilted her head back.

I took my first swipe of her sweetness. Her legs shook as my tongue licked and swirled, causing her thighs to clench. My fingers pumped in and out of her as she came apart above me. She reached down, grabbed a fistful of my hair, and hung on for dear life.

Not giving her a lot of time to come down from her climax, I sprung to my feet, grabbed her ass and lifted her so she could wrap her legs around my waist. "Where the fuck is your bedroom?"

She pointed upstairs, still panting. Once we were in her room, I kicked the door shut, spun around and slammed her into the back of the door. I stripped her of her bra and kissed her from her head to her tits, all the way to her toes and then back up to her pussy where I made her scream again.

When I stood up, Joselyn reached for my belt buckle and started to palm me through my jeans. My dick was hard enough to pound nails. I needed inside her. It had been a week too long and I wasn't waiting another fucking minute.

I placed my hand over hers that was stroking me and stopped her. In something that sounded like a groan, I partially begged, "You gotta stop, gorgeous. I want your tight pussy gripping me when I come." I reached into the back pocket of my jeans and grabbed a condom—hey, what could I say? I'd had high hopes shit would go down like this.

After rolling the rubber down myself, I slammed my mouth back onto hers and sucked her tongue into my mouth. Her hands returned to my hair and she started climbing up my body.

Nothing else existed. I had my girl naked with her legs wrapped around my hips, grinding her hot, sopping wet pussy hard on my dick. When I felt her body start to tremble, I knew she was getting ready to explode again, so I grabbed her hips and pulled her down a little harder, making sure the head of my cock hit just the right spot.

"Fuck, Paul!"

As she hit her peak, I reached between us, grabbed the base of my shaft, and slammed home. Shifting one arm at a time, I hooked my elbows under both her knees and pumped hard again.

Heaven.

Pure fucking heaven.

I had to stop or I was gonna blow way too fucking quick. After taking a breath, I leaned in again to suck the skin between her collarbone and her neck, when she started to moaned. "Still the best fucking sound, ever."

I started moving my hips in long, hard, deep thrusts using the back of the door as leverage. When she lifted her hand to find her own leverage against the nearest wall, it lined the tight pink nipple right up to my mouth. A little flick and suck was all it took. Joselyn had one hand holding the wall, and the other attempting to tug at the hair on the back of my head to keep my mouth on her tit. She turned her face up and screamed my name, the best sound that beat out all others.

Balls deep in my girl, her screaming my name and her pussy clenching down on my now oversensitive dick, I pumped a couple more times before filling the rubber.

"Fuck," I groaned. "We're gonna take a little break, and then we're going to do that again. Us taking a break killed me and I couldn't last as long as I wanted to."

"That's okay."

"I love you, Joselyn."

A tear rolled down her cheek. "I love you too, Paul."

"What's wrong?"

She started to cry a little more. "I've been waiting a long time for you to call me Joselyn and to hear you say that you love me."

I wiped her tears. "Knowing your real name doesn't change how I feel about you, gorgeous."

She nodded. "I know, but it's still nice to finally hear."

"What's your middle name?"

"Olivia."

"Joselyn Olivia Marquez, I fucking love you!"

She blushed and kissed me quickly.

"And if you want you can call me PJ." When we met, she knew me as Paul. It was weird to correct her after all this time. Now since she had a new name, it felt as though she could call me by a new name as well. After all, my close friends and the ones I loved and cared for all called me PJ.

She laughed. "Oh yeah?" I nodded. "Well, you can call me Joss."

"I'll stick to gorgeous."

"I'll stick with sexy."

I kissed her again, finally pulling out of her and carrying her to the bed. I went to clean up before crawling into bed with her.

I needed a few more minutes to build my stamina up for round two.

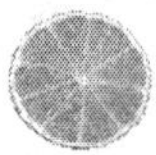

We lie wrapped in each other, my fingers lightly caressing her arm as she twirled the ring I'd finally put on her finger after we were done showing each other how much we'd *missed* one another.

I caught a glimpse of her tattoo on her side and it finally clicked:

she always had a way
with her brokenness
she would take her pieces
and make them beautiful

"Is your tattoo about that night?"

She stopped fidgeting with the ring. "For so long I felt used. I was broken." She turned over, placing her chin on my chest and peered into my eyes. "I never felt beautiful until you. I got that tattoo hoping that one day I would find my missing piece—and I have."

We kissed briefly again. There were no more words spoken. I knew what it was like to be broken and to find the missing piece. She was mine. Joss returned to staring at the ring; the afternoon sun shined through the window, reflecting the diamond against the wall.

"Can I live here?" I asked.

"I don't think so," she replied.

"Fuck."

"We'll figure it out. Maybe the case won't take that long. Can you stay with Gabe and Autumn?"

"I will until I buy us a house. Wait … after the case is over, will you live here or D.C.?"

She thought for a moment. "I wasn't planning on it, but I guess here since you have Gabe and Autumn living here and they're your best friends."

I kissed her lips. "Then yes, I'll live with them until I buy us a house. I'm sure they'll let me and if not, rent's cheap here." I laughed.

"Are you sure you're okay with me going back undercover?"

"Do I have a choice?" She shook her head. "Then I have to be. Can I be your bodyguard?"

She threw her head back and laughed. "Well, actually—"

Before she could finish, the doorbell rang.

"Who's that?" I asked.

She smiled brightly and jumped out of bed. "That's who I thought was going to be here when I answered the door and it was you."

I scrunched my eyebrows at her as she hurried and threw on clothes.

"You'll probably want to get dressed to meet him."

"Him?" I asked.

"Yep," she yelled as she ran out of the room.

I hurried and pulled on my jeans. As I walked down the stairs, I put my T-shirt back on. I could hear her laughing the closer I got, and when I turned to go into the living room, I met the eyes of a man I'd never seen before.

"Paul, this is Seth. Seth this is—"

"Her fiancé," I clarified.

He turned to her. "Fiancé?"

I pulled her to me and kissed the top of her head.

"A lot has happened since I moved to Vegas." She smiled up at me.

"Apparently." He laughed. "Well, let's pop the champagne and you two can tell me all about it before we dive into why I'm here."

The End ... for now.

Seth's story will continue in *Champagne & Handcuffs*
and will be released in 2016!

To stay up-to-date on release information, join Kimberly's newsletter!

*Turn to the back for an excerpt of
A Beautiful Kind of Love by Ellie Wade

Note from the Author

Dear Readers,

I hope you've enjoyed *Tequila & Lace* as much as I've enjoyed writing it. Getting in the mind of Paul and Joss was interesting to say the least! I'm not sure when *Champagne & Handcuffs* will be released, but please subscribe to either my blog, newsletter or both to stay up-to-date on all of my releases.

You can find the links on my website at www.authorkimberlyknight.com. You can also follow me on Facebook at facebook.com/AuthorKKnight.

I hope these two have captured a place in your heart. You can help me out by leaving a review at your favorite retailer and Goodreads. Your love and support means everything to me and I cherish you all!

Thank you again.

–Kimberly

Books by Kimberly Knight

Where I Need to Be (Club 24 Series #1)

Finding Spencer (Club 24 Series #1.5)

Wanted (Club 24 Series #2)

Wanting Spencer (Club 24 Series 2.5)

Anything Like Me (Club 24 Series #3)

Forever Spencer (Club Series 3.5)

Perfect Together – The Club 24 Series Box Set (Books 1-3.5)

Tattooed Dots (The Halo Series #1)

The One (The Halo Series #2)

Never Stop (The Halo Series #3)

My One (The Halo Series #4)

Angels & Whiskey (Saddles & Racks #1)

Tequila & Lace (Saddles & Racks #2)

Champagne & Handcuffs (Saddles & Racks #3)

And more …

Acknowledgments

First and foremost, I always need to thank my husband. For some reason, I always set a deadline and then it gets here before we know it and I'm scrambling to get my books finished. This time was no different. Thank you for being awesome and taking care of me when I was starving and needing to eat but didn't have time to cook for us. One day I'll get ahead of the game and this won't happen. I love you, you know?

To my editor, Jennifer Roberts-Hall: We're getting better! I'm so happy you're my editor and that you work with me despite my damn medical issues. You're a rockstar and without you, I would still be capitalizing babe and baby. I'm also happy to call you my friend. You're an amazing person, mother and wife and an amazing editor. I know some days you don't think you have your shit together, but we all feel that way. Pretty sure that's called life. Love you!

Renee Reigles: I don't even know where to begin. You fucking saved my ass big time with this one! Thank you from the bottom of my heart. I owe you so much. Words can't even explain how much I owe you. For all the hours you helped me and brainstormed with me… I'm pretty sure I owe you my first born. Okay, maybe not my first born, but thank you, thank you, thank you! One day I hope to have my shoulder fixed, my mojo back and to hug the ever living shit out of you! I love you, girl!

Lea Cabalar: What a crazy few months. We went from seeing each other almost every month to like never. This sucks! Thank you for always keeping up with my social media and I can't wait to hug you in LA. Actually by the time you read this, that will have already passed, but then we will have to wait until Sacramento, so damn! When you read this, think about coming to visit before Sacramento okay? I love you! #NoFilter

To my betas: Diane Robson, Heidi Eich Woodring, Jessica Griffith, Keri Anderson, Stacy Nickelson, Tiffany Chavis-Smith and Wendy O-Hara-Perry, thank you so much for taking the time out of your busy lives to get engulfed in the lives of these characters. I know beta reading is time consuming and I appreciate every minute you spent helping me to make this story what it is.

To all the bloggers who participated in my cover reveal, release day blitz and review tour, thank you! Without bloggers, I have no idea where I would be. You've all taken a chance on me and my books time and time again, and I can't tell you how much I appreciate it. I never thought I would be an author, especially one with a fan base, and I owe a lot to y'all.

To Liz Christensen of E. Marie Photography: Well, I'm pretty sure that everyone has said this is my best cover to date. You rocked it!

Emmy Hamilton: Thank you for your eyes once again. You're an awesome proof-reader!

And finally, thank you readers for believing in me and taking a chance on my books again and again. Without you guys I wouldn't still be writing and living my dream!

Photographer:

Liz Christensen

facebook.com/E.MariePhotographs

emc33photos@gmail.com

Male Cover Model:

Ryan Kurek

facebook.com/RyanKurekOfficial

Female Cover Model:

Allie Renee

facebook.com/pages/Allie-Renee/1388801751443270

About the Author

Kimberly Knight is a USA Today Bestselling Author that lives in the mountains near a lake with her loving husband and spoiled cat, Precious. In her spare time, she enjoys watching her favorite reality TV shows, watching the San Francisco Giants win World Series and the San Jose Sharks kick butt. She's also a two time desmoid tumor/cancer fighter that's made her stronger and an inspiration to her fans. Now that she lives near a lake, she plans on working on her tan and doing more outdoor stuff like watching hot guys waterski. However, the bulk of her time is dedicated to writing and reading romance and erotic fiction.

www.authorkimberlyknight.com

facebook.com/AuthorKKnight

twitter.com/Author_KKnight

pinterest.com/authorkknight

Follow her on Instagram: KimBrulee10

A BEAUTIFUL KIND OF LOVE

by

Ellie Wade

Here's the thing. Life happens. What does that even mean? Well, it means just that.

Life.

Literally.

Just.

Happens.

It is in constant motion, going on, no matter the circumstances and regardless of the outcomes. Sometimes, things happen the way we want them to, and sometimes, they don't.

In actuality, we have little control over how things turn out in the end. It is impossible to know how the choices we make will change the course of our future, how a small break from a relationship might seal our fate, or how an inconsequential choice over something we deem temporary could become permanent.

You see, every action has a reaction, and that reaction has another, and so on and on. Therefore, once that action is put out into the universe, we have no control over the infinite amount of reactions that might occur, forever changing the future.

I don't know if I believe in soul mates, but I do know that someone is out there for everyone.

There is one person who fits so perfectly in my life, someone I love unconditionally—someone who makes me laugh until I cry, and someone who I'm so attracted to that my blood will race through my veins at his every touch.

Okay, that sounds a lot like the definition of a soul mate, so maybe I do believe in it. Perhaps though, people can have more than one, but I don't.

I have one, and his name is Jax Porter.

I have known Jax my whole life, and by extension, I have loved him with every breath I've taken throughout my entire existence. Our mothers have been best friends, and Jax and I were born a mere month apart. Ever since we could communicate through slobbery gurgles, we have been put in the position to be inseparable best friends.

So, one might think our story is sealed, our fate written.

Unfortunately, that's not how it works. Through this experience of life, we have many choices to make, and each one will lead us down another path.

I find myself at a destination that I never imagined, and to be honest, I am terrified of it.

Yet here I am.

Now, I have to figure out where to go from here.

Prologue

Age Twelve

I turn my face, laughing, as a gush of water collides with my cheek. Wiping the wet drops from my eyes, I see Jax surfacing from his recent cannonball.

"That was a big one, right?" His smile is wide with enthusiasm.

"Yeah, it was okay," I tease. "I bet mine will be bigger!"

I swim toward the ladder of our pool, taking note that the normally bright blue liner underneath the rippling water is taking on more of a greenish hue than normal. I love our pool in the humid Michigan summers, but I hate cleaning it. I sigh inwardly, remembering that it's my week to vacuum the pool. *Yuck.* Maybe I can bribe my younger sister, Keeley, to do it for me. She is usually pretty easy to win over. Admittedly, she sucks slightly more than I do when it comes to cleaning our algae-happy pool, so perhaps that isn't such a good idea.

"Sure, *Little.* Give it your best shot!" Jax grins as he flexes his arm muscles, displaying his manly biceps.

I grab on to the ladder and pull myself up, shaking my head, with a big grin spread across my face. He always makes me laugh. He has been my best friend for as long as I can remember.

Our mothers have been best friends since they were young. They grew up as next-door neighbors, and because they were each the only child in their families, they were more like sisters. They were each pregnant at the same time with Jax and me. So, we have been thrown together since we were born—or at least a month after I was born since I am a month older than Jax.

"Hey, it's Lil, not Little!" I say in reference to Jax's love of switching my nickname as a joke. "And remember, 'Though she be but little, she is fierce.'" The framed Shakespeare quote has adorned my bedroom wall for several years. It was a birthday present from Jax's mom, Susie.

The Little jokes are just that—jokes. I'm not abnormally small for my age. Well, I was one of the smallest girls in the sixth grade, but I know that in a month, come seventh grade, I am going to shoot up. At least I hope I will.

Usually, my size doesn't bother me, but I was the last girl in my class to get my period, and that was embarrassing. I wear a training bra, but to be honest, I don't even need it. I've got nothing. My older sister, Amy, is fifteen, and she has had legitimate boobs since she was twelve.

I steal a glance at her sitting in the lounge chair on the side of the pool, reading her Kindle. She looks like Mom in her bikini. She has hips and everything.

I still wear my purple one-piece. I refuse to wear a bikini. It would only draw attention to my wimpy boy body, not that it matters. Other than the few snide comments the bratty girls in my class have made, it doesn't affect me that I have no curves whatsoever.

I get a running start off of the diving board, and thinking big and heavy thoughts for maximum splash effect, I jump as high as I can before grabbing my legs and crashing my balled-up body into the water with what I'm sure is an epic splash.

When I surface, Jax calls out, "Seven, max. Maybe even a six and a half."

"No way!" I protest. "That was at least a nine!" I tread water as I wipe the drops from my eyes. "What do you think, Kee Kee?" I direct my question to my nine-year-old sister.

She is adjusting her face mask and snorkel. She has been practicing her snorkeling abilities nonstop lately.

Her eyes appear bigger, showcased through the thick plastic of the hot-pink face mask she's wearing. She spits the snorkel out of her mouth. "I don't know, Lily. I wasn't really watching." She shrugs her shoulders.

"That doesn't matter, Keeley! You should always side with me. I'm your sister!"

She shrugs again before placing her face in the water to resume her snorkeling.

Jax chuckles. "Ah, poor little Lily. Can't get your sister to cheat for you? As I said, six and a half."

"Hey, mister, you said seven first! You are not taking it back. Besides, I give yours a five!"

He slaps his hand through the water, sending a wave into my face. "You're a sore loser, Lil."

"No, I'm not because I didn't lose. You got a five," I say indignantly. I swim to the front of the pool where I can stand.

Jax follows. He grabs my hands in his, entwining his fingers through mine. "Name That Tune?"

I grin. "Okay. You go first."

Hands intertwined, we take a deep breath and let our bodies sink into the water. With our heads submerged, Jax begins to belt out a song under the water. I listen really closely because it is very difficult to hear the song through the water. It reminds me of what that teacher from Charlie Brown would sound like if she were singing.

We run out of breath and come up for air.

"Any guesses?" he asks.

"Hmm. It sounded like Whitney Houston's 'I Will Always Love You.'"

"Huh?" Utter confusion is etched across his face. "I have no idea what song you're talking about."

"I know you have heard that song before!"

"No, Lily, I haven't," he answers seriously.

"It is a classic. Haven't you ever watched *The Bodyguard*?"

"Body what?"

"*The Bodyguard.* It's an old movie with Whitney Houston and that other actor guy." I love to watch all my mom's old movies.

"Lily, seriously. Guess a song that I would actually know."

I let out a sigh. "Fine, but it sounded exactly like that song."

"Um, no, it didn't. Now, give me a real guess." He smirks.

"That was a real guess, but fine. Let me think. 'Get the Party Started' by Pink."

He laughs. "No. It sounded nothing like that."

"Fine, I give up. What song were you singing?" I remove my hands from his and cross my arms as I pout.

"Work It by Missy Elliot."

"What?" I ask in confusion.

"I heard it on Landon's iPod, and it's about sex, I think."

I cover my mouth in a gasp before hitting him on the chest. "Ew! Why would I know about that song? That's gross! Does your mom know that Landon listens to that type of music?"

"He's seventeen. I'm sure my mom doesn't care. Anyway, the song is funny. Lighten up."

"Gross. No, I'm never going to listen to a song about that. That is disgusting, and you shouldn't be listening to it either. Plus, you have to pick a song that I'd know, or this game is stupid." I resume my crossed-arms, pouty position.

He chuckles. "Okay, fine. Your turn. The same goes for you—pick a song that I'd know."

"Okay. Ready?" Releasing my arms from my display of irritation, I grab a hold of his hands, and we go under the water once more.

After we've gone through six songs and six unsuccessful guesses, my mom brings out a tray of food and beverages and places it on the patio table under the shade of the umbrella.

"Kiddos, lemonade and chicken salad pitas are ready. You must be hungry."

"Thanks, Mom," I say as I climb out of the pool.

"Thanks, Miranda," he addresses my mom as he follows behind me.

"Jax, your mom texted me a while back. Landon will be over to pick you up in an hour. Your dad's benefit is tonight, and you have to go home to get ready."

He groans. "Ugh. Seriously? Did she say if I could bring Lil?"

"I don't think so, honey. I think your dad just wants you and Landon there today."

"This sucks." He plops down in a lawn chair and takes a big bite of the pita sandwich.

Mr. Porter is the CEO of a big advertising firm in Kalamazoo that's about forty minutes away from here. The firm seems to always have some dinner or event that requires the Porter family to dress up. Jax hates it, but he hates it less when I'm allowed to tag along. When I go, we manage to make it fun.

We live in the country, outside of the small town of Athens—and I'm talking, a one-blinking-red-light-in-the-center-of-town small. We have one gas station, a bar, a family-owned ice cream place, and that's about all.

Jax's dad is probably one of the most successful people in our town, and although they are good people, his parents carry themselves with an air of superiority, especially his dad. My dad is a lawyer, working in the same city as Mr. Porter, but I'd say our family is more easygoing.

I grab a pita and a glass of lemonade, and I collapse onto the lounge chair next to Jax. "It won't be that bad." I nudge him with my shoulder.

He gives me an unenthusiastic grunt and finishes his pita in four bites. "Well, I have an hour. What do you want to do? Play Mario?"

"No. I don't want to be inside. Ride bikes?" I ask.

"Yeah, that's cool."

My mom approaches me with a metal aerosol can in hand. "Lily, let me spray you again with sunscreen."

I stand without argument and put my arms out, preparing for the SPF onslaught. Even though I just lathered up over an hour ago, I know better than to question my mom when it comes to my skin protection. I am engulfed in an SPF cloud smelling of coconut and chemicals.

"Okay, let me get your face with the lotion."

"Mom, I can wipe lotion on my face," I say. I turn toward her and watch her lather up her hands with the greasy cream.

"I know, honey. I just want to make sure you're good and protected. The sun is hot today."

I have a light splattering of freckles across the brim of my nose, which my dad insists is the cutest part about me. If it weren't for my mom's commitment to skincare, I would probably be covered in them. I'm definitely the most fair-skinned person in my family. My mom and Keeley have blonde hair and blue eyes as well, but both their skin and hair are slightly darker than mine.

"All right, Jax. Let me get you now."

"I'm fine. Really, Miranda," he protests.

"Nope. Your skin needs protection, too. Come here, you."

I giggle at his expression as my mom rubs sunscreen onto his face. He is definitely the opposite of me with his raven hair and olive skin.

His emerald eyes look mildly annoyed as he turns away from my mom. "Ready?"

"Ready, Freddy!"

"Don't forget your helmets!" my mom yells as we make our way toward the garage.

I wave my arm in acknowledgment of her directive.

We pedal along the country road that weaves between expansive cornfields. The cornstalks are taller than me now, which is an indication that summer will soon come to an end and we will welcome our seventh grade year.

"What do you want to do for your birthday this year?" he calls out as we glide speedily down a hill.

"I don't know. What do you think?"

Both our families make a big deal of birthdays, throwing extravagant parties.

"Well, thirteen is, like, an important one, isn't it? I'm sure your mom is going to go all out."

My birthday is at the end of August, right before school starts up. "Not sure if I want a huge party this year. Maybe I should just do something with you and my family."

"What about all our friends from school?"

"Meh," I let out an uninterested sound.

Sure, I have friends at school, but Jax is my best friend, and he's the only one who really matters.

"Come on. You don't want to invite our whole class and have a giant bash? We could have a bonfire outside and put on music for dancing. Maybe we could play Spin the Bottle or something. You're going to be thirteen. Don't thirteen-year-olds do stuff like that?"

"Jax! What has gotten into you today? First, songs about dirty stuff, and now, kissing? I'm not letting our whole class put their germy mouths on mine. Ew. No, thank you. Dinner and a movie, it is!"

He throws his head back and laughs. "You're a prude sometimes, Miss Lily Madison. I feel bad for the first guy who tries to date you."

"You're being so weird right now. I think we both have a while to worry about that."

"I've been thinking about asking Katie Phelps out."

Katie is one of the most popular girls in our class. I'm not sure how much that is saying, considering we go to such a small school and our class consists of sixty kids. I think of her as a friend, but she can be bossy sometimes.

"Really? How does that even work? You are too young to date." I feel tightness in my chest that I can't quite explain.

"Yeah. Well, obviously, I wouldn't literally take her out, but we would talk on the phone and see each other at school. We could have our parents drop us off at the movies or something, too. You and I do that all the time."

"I know, but that is different. We are friends. Will your parents really let you hang out with a girl you like?"

"I don't know. I guess I'll see."

"Well, when would we hang out?"

I don't want to share Jax. He's too good for Katie anyway.

"We would hang out like normal. That wouldn't change." He

sounds sure.

"Yeah, it'd better not," I say with authority.

"You're silly. Come on. Let's head back."

I nod, knowing that Landon is going to be at my house shortly to get Jax.

We pedal back to my house in relative silence. I'm lost in my thoughts, wondering why he wants to date. It seems kinda odd to me. If I'm honest with myself, I'm nervous. Jax has been my partner in crime since we could crawl. I don't want to share him, not yet.

I change my mind on things a lot, but Jax is the one thing I'm sure of. He's my best friend, and I'm not letting him go.

Chapter One

Five Years Later

I scan the crowded stands for my friend Kristyn as I walk toward the packed seats. Everyone from our town came out for tonight's football game against our rival school. I stop a moment in front of the concession stand near the chain-link fence surrounding the football field and watch the band's preshow. The cheerleaders are in sync with the music as they dance on the track that circles the field. They are wearing their skirts today due to the unseasonably warm autumn air. I love Friday night football games on our home field, especially when the weather isn't awful.

"Lily!"

I hear my name and turn to see Kristyn waving at me from the third row. I wave back and make my way toward her.

I shuffle my way in front of the seated people, inching closer to Kristyn in the center of the row.

"Hey." I smile when I reach her. "Sorry I'm late." I don't offer up an excuse because I don't have one. Sometimes, I'm not always the most punctual person. Even though I was supposed to meet Kristyn in the parking lot twenty minutes ago, I'm just proud of myself that I made it here well before kickoff.

"No worries." She smiles warmly at me.

Kristyn is my closest friend at school besides Jax. She is great and would do anything for me. I adore her.

I look out onto the field in search of him. I know it sounds silly, but I feel his stare on me. I catch his gaze as he stands there, all padded up while holding the football to his chest. I wave, grinning enthusiastically, before giving him a thumbs-up. He shakes his head, and his eyes shine with humor. Though I can't hear him, I know he chuckles before turning away from me, throwing the football to another player.

Jax has been the varsity starting quarterback since last year. It is unusual for a sophomore to start on varsity, especially as the quarterback, but when it comes to Jax, I'm not surprised. He is naturally talented at most things. He gets great grades with minimal effort and has excelled at every sport he's attempted.

"How is Jax feeling about the game?" Kristyn asks.

"Good. I think he is confident that we'll win tonight."

I focus on his arm muscles as they flex with every throw. He truly is a hot specimen, and I can totally understand why every girl here—and from the surrounding schools, for that matter—is all gaga over him.

"Well, the other team is undefeated so far this season," Kristyn notes.

"Yeah, so are we. I'm not worried."

My leg is forcefully pushed to the side, and I pull it back and look up to see Maeve, Jax's current girlfriend, walking in front of me.

"Oh, I'm sorry, *Lily*," Maeve says with a voice that shows anything but. She puts emphasis on my name, and it sounds vile coming from her mouth.

I grin reluctantly, acknowledging her pseudo-apology, and wrap my arms around my shins, holding my legs out of harm's way, while she and her posse continue their way across the row to the seats at the end.

Kristyn leans over and whispers in my ear, "Have you told Jax about her yet?"

I shake my head, indicating that I haven't.

"Why not? He would never be with her if he knew she was such a bitch to you."

I turn toward Kristyn. "He will figure it out on his own. He always does," I say in a low voice.

"No, you should really tell him, Lily."

"There will always be bitches in this world, Kristyn. They don't bother me too much. I just ignore them." I shrug.

"Promise me, if she ever crosses the line, you will tell him." Her voice is heavy with concern.

"I promise." But as I say it, I know that it will never come to that.

Jax will discover Maeve's true character before I have to say anything. I didn't know Maeve much before she and Jax started dating about a month ago. She is a senior, and we didn't have too much contact with each other prior to this year. I'm not surprised that she is rude to me. Many of his girlfriends in the past have been as well. They always start out cool, but I think jealousy eventually kicks in when they realize how close he and I actually are, and then the claws come out. Jealousy really isn't attractive on anyone.

It seems that Jax has had a girlfriend of some sort pretty much since seventh grade, but I will say that it hasn't affected our relationship too much. Our friendship is solid, and he puts me first. It's not like I've asked him to choose between his girlfriend and me because I haven't, and I would never ask him to. He values our friendship and always makes time for us. As soon as he notices a girl's jealousness or rudeness toward me, he ends the relationship without a second thought.

The game is exhilarating the entire way through. The two teams go back and forth, but we come out a touchdown ahead. I love watching Jax in his element, and I'm so proud of him. The guys are going wild on the field, raising their fists in triumph.

I'm happy we won, especially because having to hang out with the guys tonight after a loss would have been a complete downer. There is a big bonfire in a secluded field on a classmate's property. Those of us from small town Michigan might not be known for much, but we have sweet-ass bonfires.

I watch as the players exit the field and head toward the doors leading to the locker room. Jax breaks away from the line of rowdy football players and jogs toward me. I stand and leave the bleachers, followed by Kristyn. I weave my way through the celebration to meet him halfway.

He pulls me into a sweaty hug, squeezing me with a fierce intensity.

"Great game!" I congratulate him.

"Thanks! Wait for me, and you can ride with me to the field." He pulls away and locks me in his intense stare.

"It's okay. I'm going to catch a ride with Kristyn. I will meet you there."

He skeptically looks at me. "Are you sure?"

I smile. "Yes, I'm sure. I will see you there, okay?"

He pauses for a moment. "Okay."

"Good game. Seriously, I'm so proud of you, Jax."

"Thanks, Little. See you soon." He uses his personal nickname for me.

It stems from when he was a toddler. He thought my mom was calling me Little when she was saying Lil, and it has stuck. I used to hate it when I was younger, but I love it now.

I hear the shrill tone of Maeve's voice calling out Jax's name behind me, and I give Kristyn a subtle look. We leave Jax and make our way toward the parking lot.

I bounce off the seat in the cab of Kristyn's pickup truck as we careen down the bumpy path to the field. As we get closer, I see the huge fire already well ablaze. Logs and bales of hay are positioned around the fire, forming a circle around the flames. Another larger ring of hay bales is around the first one, creating two seating areas facing the bonfire. Poles are positioned in equal distances from each other between the two circles. Little white Christmas lights are strung from one pole to the next, surrounding the seating areas in a blanket of soft white light. Beyond the twinkling lights are the outskirts of the field surrounded by dark woods. Music is pounding with deep bass coming from the speakers positioned in the back of someone's rusty Ford F-150.

After we park in the line of cars at the edge of the woods, we head toward the fire.

"It's going to be a crazy one with that win tonight," Kristyn says.

"Yeah, I figure it will be." I scan over the crowd of my schoolmates already congregating with red Solo cups in their hands. "Do you want to find the keg? I can drive you home if you want to drink."

I'm not much of a beer fan. I know they say it is an acquired taste, but I don't think I will ever acquire it. It tastes bitter and dreadful to me.

"No, I'm good. I don't feel like drinking tonight," she responds.

"Yeah, me neither, especially something that tastes like pee." I scrunch up my nose.

She giggles. "Exactly."

I hear my name and turn to find Alden heading in our direction.

Alden is a great guy. We have several classes together. His grandfather owns this land that we are on. He has been increasingly friendly with me lately, and I get the impression that he likes me. I'm not a very good judge of that sort of thing though. I haven't ever had a boyfriend, but I admit that I haven't put any effort into getting one. My life is pretty full with my family activities, studying, my friends, and Jax. Unlike Jax, I actually have to study hard for my good grades. It's only the fall of my junior year, so I don't feel like I'm missing out on the high school relationship deal yet. I have time.

Alden closes the gap between us and hugs me. He releases me before pulling Kristyn into one. Letting go of Kristyn, he turns to me, "So glad you could make it. Can I get you something to drink?"

"No, we're good. Thanks though." I smile up at him, and I take note of how close we are standing.

I bet I could feel his breath against my face if I leaned in a fraction more. I am terrified to do so. It probably smells like beer or something else unappealing. It's better to imagine it in a positive light.

I'm spoiled with Jax. He is the only guy my age who gets this close to me, and he always smells wonderful. I know it sounds cliché, but he really is walking perfection. Any guy I date is going to have big shoes to fill. Jax and I aren't like that, but I know I will inadvertently compare everyone to him. He is what I know.

"Come on. A group of us are over there." Alden nods toward the seating area.

"Sure," I agree.

He places his hand against the small of my back and leads me to the warmth of the crackling flames. We are making our way around the fire and in the direction of the bales he indicated when I hear Jax.

"Lil!"

I stop walking and pivot on one foot in the direction from where we just came. I'm met by Jax's open arms as he pulls me into a hug.

"Have you been here long?"

"No, we actually just got here," I reply.

"Oh, good. Hey, I have to go talk to Paul. You coming?"

"Um, sure. Just let me…" I look behind me to speak to Alden, but he is no longer there.

My eyes skim the faces congregated around the fire, all cast in a warm golden hue, and I spot him on the opposite side of us, speaking with some friends. He raises his head to meet my stare and smiles shyly, giving me an upward nod, before returning to his conversation.

"Okay, never mind. Let's go."

Kristyn and I hang out with Jax and most of the football team for the majority of the night.

Maeve showed up shortly after Jax, and she has been draped all over him ever since. She really does annoy me to no end. It's not jealousy I feel but simple irritation with her obnoxious behavior.

I contemplate expanding my social circle, and I go to talk to others, but I don't venture too far away from Jax. I never do. Maybe it is the fact that he has been close to me from the moment he was born, but I feel unsettled when I'm too far away from him.

As the night wears on, the gathering thins, and the random groups of people sporadically positioned around the fire come together to become one single crowd.

"Hey."

I hear Alden's voice at the same time I feel his hand on my arm. I turn to him. His eyelids appear heavy as if he is concentrating on keeping them open.

I chuckle as he sways. "How's the beer?" I ask, motioning to the red cup full of sloshing liquid in his hand.

"Good! Can I get you some?"

I shake my head. "No, I'm still good. Thanks."

Letting go of my arm, he lifts his free hand and takes a strand of my hair in his fingers. He studies it before he tucks it behind my ear. Despite his obvious inebriated state, the gesture is sweet, and I'm mesmerized as I watch him take in my face.

"You're so pretty, Lily."

"Alden."

Jax's voice comes from behind me, and I jump, startled. The trance that drunken sweet Alden had me under is shattered.

"Oh, hey, man," Alden addresses Jax. "See ya, Lil." He smiles weakly before he turns to someone beside me and starts up a conversation.

I take a few steps away from Alden before addressing Jax, "What was that all about?"

"What?" he asks innocently.

"Um…that"—I motion to Alden—"thing between you and him. You ran him off."

Jax nods. "He was hitting on you."

My eyebrows rise. "So?"

He shrugs. "He's not good enough for you."

I sigh. "That's what you say about every guy. Alden's really nice."

"He's drunk," Jax says matter-of-factly.

"Yeah, and so are most of the people here. Who cares?"

"I do."

"You have to stop scaring away every guy who wants to talk to me. You're worse than my dad."

Jax feigns innocence. "I only do that to the ones who aren't worth your time."

I scrunch my lips into a pout and look up to Jax in annoyance before answering, "Apparently, that is every boy in our high school."

“Basically, yeah,” he agrees. “Don’t be mad.” He pulls me into a hug and kisses the top of my head.

“I’m not. It would be nice to expand my friendship circle, is all. You can’t always be around, Jax.”

“For you, Lily, I can. I’m always here for you. You know that.” He kisses me again on top of my head before he is yanked away.

“Jax! I miss you,” Maeve whines. She has become increasingly drunk as the night has progressed, as evident by her speech morphing into one long slurred mess and the decibel of her voice passing the point of obnoxiously loud.

Vomit explodes from Maeve’s mouth onto the grass in front of his feet.

“Whoa!” Jax yells, jumping back. “Damn!” He makes his way behind Maeve to steady her as she expels everything from her stomach.

Becca, Maeve’s best friend, steps beside Jax. “Seriously?” I hear the annoyance in her voice. “I will take her home.”

Becca glares at the now dry-heaving mess. Maeve is bent over with her arms propped on her knees as she coughs toward the ground.

“Are you sure?” Jax asks, appearing concerned.

I know that he is trying to camouflage his relief.

Becca wraps her arms around Maeve’s waist. “Yeah, I got her. It’s finc.” Shc lcads Maeve toward the line of vehicles parked up against the tree line.

I turn to Kristyn. She is smirking in the direction of the retreating girls. She briefly shakes her head and then steps closer to me.

“I think I’m actually going to get going, too. Do you want me to take you home?" she asks.

Before I can answer, Jax says from behind me, "I got her. Thanks, Kristyn."

We say our good-byes, and I turn toward Jax.

"So, is it going to be refrigerator exploration or Denny's?" he asks, leaning in close to my face.

When we are together on weekend nights, we usually hang out and have a late-night meal. We either hunt through the refrigerator at one of our homes to see what yummy leftovers await, or we drive thirty minutes to the next town where a Denny's is open twenty-four hours.

"I think it is a Denny's kind of night."

He flashes me his all-American boy smile. "I agree. Let's get out of here."

Grabbing my cell from my back pocket, I shoot my mom a text, letting her know I'm going to eat with Jax and will be home late. As long as I'm with Jax and keep her posted on our plans, I don't have a curfew. She adores him and completely trusts him.

I love our late-night dinner dates. Jax and I spend a lot of time together, but the older we get, the less uninterrupted quality time we have. We can spend hours talking and laughing at Denny's, and we have many times. We never run out of things to say. He is my favorite person in this world to be with.

Now, the only question is, what am I going to order tonight? I'm always so indecisive. I could go with sweet and get French toast or savory and get a burrito. Or I could do something different altogether.

"So, what are you in the mood for tonight?" Jax asks in an amused tone.

I chuckle. I swear, he can read my mind sometimes.

I shake my head. "I'm torn. I don't know."

"Okay, give me your options, and we'll go over the pros and cons of each."

Giggling, I begin to tell him my meal choices, and so begins our twenty-minute conversation on what I should order. As I said, we can talk about anything.

Get *A Beautiful Kind of Love* by Ellie Wade today
to read the rest!

Made in the USA
Middletown, DE
20 March 2016